Robert Greene, Alexander Balloch Grosart

Green Pastures

Being choice extracts from the works of Robert Greene, M.A., of both universities,

1560(?)-1592

Robert Greene, Alexander Balloch Grosart

Green Pastures
*Being choice extracts from the works of Robert Greene, M.A., of both universities,
1560(?)-1592*

ISBN/EAN: 9783337426422

Printed in Europe, USA, Canada, Australia, Japan

Cover: Foto ©Andreas Hilbeck / pixelio.de

More available books at **www.hansebooks.com**

Green Pastures:

Being Choice Extracts from
the Works of Robert Greene,
M.A., of both Univerſities
1560(?)-1592. Made by
Alexander B.
Groſart

LONDON
ELLIOT STOCK, 62, Paternoster Row
1894

INTRODUCTION.

FROM an Author ſo voluminous that his collective 'Life and Works' extend to no fewer than fifteen conſiderable volumes (in the 'Huth Library'), the difficulty has not been to find materials for a volume of our Elizabethan Library, but what to ſelect. For example, it was very ſoon diſcovered that ſome of his moſt characteriſtic writings muſt be left abſolutely untouched, inaſmuch as any one, e.g., of the Coney-catching Series, or of the Autobiographical Series, would alone over-flow into two or more ſuch volumes, ſo matter-ful are they, and ſo impoſſible is it to repreſent their higheſt qualities by brief extracts. In reluctantly but inevitably leaving theſe aſide, I venture to ſay that no books contain more vivid word-pictures of Engliſh low-life in the reign of Elizabeth than do theſe. They are bitten in with marvellous Dutch-

like minuteneſs of touch. As for his perſonal narratives of penitence and confeſſion, I for one do not envy the man who can read them with unwet eyes. There is a burning truth, a pathetic integrity, a weird power about them that neighbour theſe ſadly little known books with De Quincey's ' Confeſſions,' and reduce to commonplace thoſe of Rouſſeau. The letters and appeals to his wife and evil aſſociates thrill to-day the moſt fiſh-blooded reader. Only ſuch a ghoul as Gabriel Harvey could doubt their ſincerity. I indulge the hope that ſome readers of theſe words of mine, and of this booklet, will be ſtirred to ſeek acceſs to the following (their title-pages ſummarily given):

1. CONEY-CATCHING SERIES.

(a) *A notable Diſcovery of cooſnage now daily praĉtiſed by ſundry lewd perſons called Connie-catchers and Croſſe-biters* . . . 1591.

(b) *The ſecond parte* . . . 1591.

(c) *The thirde parte* . . . *with the new deviſed knaviſh art of Foole-taking* . . . 1592.

(*d*) *A Difputation between a Hee Conny-Catcher and a Shee Conny-Catcher . . .* 1592.

(*e*) *The Black Bookes Meffenger, laying open the Life and Death of Ned Browne, one of the moft notable Cutpurfes, Crofs-biters and Conny-catchers that ever lived in England . . .* 1592. *Then muft be read* (*Works, vol. xi., pp.* 39-104) *the attack on above books.*

(*f*) *The Defence of Conny-catching, or a Confutation of thofe two injurious Pamphlets, publifhed by* R. G., *againft the practioners of many nimble-witted and myftical Sciences . . .* 1592.

2. AUTOBIOGRAPHICAL SERIES.

(*g*) *Green's Groat's-worth of Wit, bought with a Million of Repentance . . .* 1592.

(*h*) *The Repentance of Robert Greene, Mafter of Artes . . .* 1592.

(*i*) *Greene's Vifion, written at the inftant of his death . . .* 1592.

To thefe muft be added his numerous

Epiſtles-dedicatory and prefatory. They have all perſonal alluſions of the moſt intereſting ſort. I ſhould gladly have brought them together. I have been compelled to limit myſelf to a ſingle example—the Epiſtle-dedicatory to 'Perimides the Blackſmith.' There is exceptional graciouſness and daintineſs of phraſing in all his Epiſtles.

After excluſion (ſpeaking broadly) of the whole of theſe, there remain materials for at leaſt five ſeparate volumes equal to the preſent.

(*a*) APOPHTHEGMS AND APT SAYINGS, many of them long paſſed into proverbs, albeit certain were probably contemporary proverbs that were worked into the ſeveral books. Our few 'handfuls of purpoſe' will demonſtrate how full a harveſt might have been reaped in this field.

(*b*) THE PLAYS. *Eheu! eheu!* We have the mere 'flotſam and jetſam' of his prolific pen 'for the theatre.' But in the two volumes of his Works (xiii. and xiv.) his four ſurviving Plays abound in 'brave *tranflunary things.'* We have *ftriven* to prefent typical fpecimens. It was our good fortune to be the firft to reclaim the extremely remarkable play of 'Selimus' for Greene.

(c) MANNERS, CUSTOMS, FASHIONS, *games and fports, fuperftitions, town and country ongoings, odd characters, feafts and feftivals, etc., etc., find all but inexhauftible illuftration in thefe pre-eminently manners-painting books.* One wonders that *fo* full a quarry has been *fo* little worked. Compilers might have made their meagre pages rich from almoft any one of the volumes enumerated. See vol. xv. of *Works*—Gloffarial Index —*fpecial lifts, etc., etc.;* alfo under 'Actors and Players' in the prefent volume, which, à la France, are to be read between the lines.

Within our narrow limits we have (it is believed) furnifhed enough to make it clear that young Greene was no merely grotefque rival to young William Shakefpeare. It *lies on the surface that if only the 'wrecked life' had found a friend and helper in his (later) mighty contemporary, that is if co-operation had been sought—not antagonism —English literature should have been the certain gainer. We are so used to idolatrize Shakespeare because of his simply incomparable genius, that we shirk inquiring into his relations with his precursors and contemporaries. I for one feel satisfied that fuller knowledge of these would prove that for years, when feeling his way upward, Shakespeare was a very buccaneer in 'spoiling the Egyptians,' or unmetaphorically in turning to his own account the MS. writings of unfortunate contemporaries who were constrained to write for the theatres. On these and cognate matters I must refer the reader to Professor Storojenko's 'Life' of Greene, with our annotations, which form vol. i. of the Works.*

I would specially commend the L'Allegro and Penseroso-like bursts of musical song that will be found in this volume. The (*so-called*) *Paſtorals have exquiſite touches and fineſt-wrought rhyme and rhythm. The Love-ſongs are tender and paſſionate. The 'comic vein' is genuine. His patriotic ſtanding-up for the 'common people' (e.g., in 'The Pinner of Wakefield') is hiſtorically moſt noticeable. Altogether I ſhall be diſappointed if our 'Green Paſtures'—the pun being permiſſible, as was Spurgeon's 'Stones from Ancient Brooks' (= Thomas Brooks, the Puritan)—be not welcomed as a pleaſant ſurpriſe to be placed beſide our 'Bower of Delight' of* NICOLAS BRETON.

I cloſe with a quotation from myſelf— 'I muſt take this freſh opportunity of recalling that as the converſe of Herrick's famous (or infamous) pleading, that if his verſe were impure, his life was chaſte, Greene's writings are exceptionally clean. Nor muſt he be refuſed the benefit of this in any judicial eſtimate of him. It is equally harſh and uncritical to ſay that this confeſſedly diſſolute-living man wrote purely becauſe it paid him to do ſo. It did no ſuch thing.

It would have paid, and did pay, to write impurely, and as ministering to the unchaste appetite of readers for garbage. To his undying honour, Robert Greene,—equally with James Thomson,—left scarce a line that dying he need have wished " to blot." I can't understand the nature of anyone who can think hardly of Greene in the light of his ultimate penitence and absolute confession. It is (if the comparison be not over-bold) as though one had taunted David with his sin after the 51st Psalm' (Editor's Introduction to Life: Works, i., pp. xix-xx).

A. B. G.

CONTENTS.

ABATEMENTS.

THE ftiffeft metal yieldeth to the ftamp,
the ftrongeft oak to the carpenter's axe,
the hard fteel to the file, and the ftouteft
heart doth bow when Nature bids him
bend. . . . There is no adamant fuch
which the blood of a goat cannot make
foft, no tree fo found which the fcarab
fly will not pierce, no iron fo hard which
ruft will not fret, no mortal thing fo
fure which Time will not confume, nor
no man fo valiant which cometh not
without excufe when Death doth call.
The phœnix hath black pens as well as
gliftering feathers, the pureft wine hath
his lees, the luckieft year hath his cani-
cular days.   Venus had a mole in her
face, and Adonis a fcar upon his chin.
There was fometimes thunder heard in
the Temple of Peace, and Fortune is
never fo favourable but fhe is as fickle:

B

her profperity is ever fauced with the four drops of adverfity, being conftant in nothing but in inconftancy. Scipio efcaped many foreign broils, but, returning home in triumph, was flain with a tile. Cæfar conquered the whole world, yet was cowardly flain in the Senate. So Bonfadio. . . . (Morando : the 'Tritameron of Love' [1517], iii., pp. 51, 52.)

ABOMINABLE, ABHOMIN-ABLE.

The defire of his fond affection fo blinded his underftanding that he paufed not to pervert both human and Divine laws for the accomplifhment thereof : no rules of reafon, no fear of laws, no pricks of confcience, no refpect of honefty, no regard of God or man, could prohibit him from his peftiferous purpofe : for if laws had been of force, he knew his deed was contrary to all laws, in violating his facred oath ; of confcience, he knew it terrible ; of honefty, he knew it moft wicked ; of

God or man, he knew it abominable in the fight of both ('Mamillia' [1583], ii., p. 118). [Nares annotates on this word : 'A pedantic affectation of more correct fpeaking, founded upon a falfe notion of the etymology ; fuppofing it to be from *ab homine* inftead of *abominor,* which is the true derivative. Shake-fpeare has ridiculed this affectation in the character of the pedant Holofernes : "They are *abhominable,* which he [Don Armado] would call abominable" ("Love's Labour's Loft," v., 1). But it was not neceffarily pedantic fo to fpell. As fimple matter of fact, the word carried in it for long meanings corre-fpondent with the double derivation.— G.]

ACTORS AND ACTING.*

So highly were Comedies efteemed in thofe days [of Terence and Plautus in Rome], that men of great honour and grave account were the actors, the Senate and the confuls continually pre-fent as auditors at all fuch fports,

* See Introduction.

rewarding the author with rich rewards,
according to the excellency of the
Comedy. Thus continued this faculty
famous, till covetoufnefs crept into the
quality, and that mean men, greedy of
gains, did fall to practife the acting of
fuch plays, and in the theatre prefented
their Comedies, but to fuch only as re-
warded them well for their pains. When
thus Comedians grew to be mercenaries,
then men of accompt left to practife
fuch paftimes, and difdained to have
their honours blemifhed with the ftain
of fuch bafe and vile gains : infomuch
that both Comedies and Tragedies grew
to lefs accompt in Rome, in that the
free fight of fuch fports was taken away
by covetous defires ; yet the people (who
are delighted with fuch novelties and
paftimes) made great refort, paid largely
and highly applauded their doings, infomuch that the Actors, by continual
ufe, grew not only excellent but rich
and infolent. Amongft whom in the
days of Tully one Rofcius grew to be of
fuch exquifite perfection in his faculty,
that he offered to contend with the
orators of that time in gefture, as they
did in eloquence ; boafting that he could

exprefs a paffion in as many fundry actions as Tully could difcourfe it in variety of phrafes : yea, fo proud he grew by the daily applaufe of people, that he looked for honour and reverence to be done him in the ftreets : which felf-conceit when Tully entered into with a piercing infight, he quipped at in this manner.

It chanced that Rofcius and he met at a dinner, both guefts unto Archias the poet, where the proud Comedian dared to make comparifon with Tully ; which infolency made the learned orator to grow into thefe terms : 'Why, Rofcius, art thou proud with Æfop's crow, being pranked with the glory of other's feathers? Of thyfelf thou canft fay nothing, and if the cobler hath taught thee to say *Ave Cæfar*, difdain not thy tutor becaufe thou prateft in a king's chamber. What fentence thou uttereft on the ftage, flows from the cenfure of our wits, and what fentence or conceit of the invention the people applaud for excellent, that comes from the fecrets of our knowledge. I grant your action, though it be a kind of mechanical labour, yet well done 'tis worthy of praife ; but you worthlefs, if for fo fmall a toy you wax proud.'

At this Rofcius waxed red and be-wrayed his imperfection with filence ; but this check of Tully could not keep others from the blemifh of that fault, for it grew to a general vice amongft the Actors, to excell in pride as they did exceed in excellence, and to brave it in the ftreets as they brag it on the ftage : fo that they revelled it in Rome in fuch coftly robes, that they feemed rather men of great patrimony than fuch as lived by the favour of the people. Which Publius Servilius very well noted ; for he, being the fon of a fenator and a man very valiant, met on a day with a player in the ftreets richly apparelled, who fo far forgat himfelf that he took the wall of the young nobleman ; which Servilius taking in difdain, counterchecked with this frump: ' My friend (quoth he), be not fo brag of thy filken robes, for I faw them but yefterday make a great fhow in a broker's fhop.' At this the one was afhamed and the other fmiled, and they which heard the quip laughed at the folly of the one and the wit of the other. Thus, fir,

have you heard my opinion briefly of
plays, that Menander devifed them for
the fuppreffing of vanities : neceffary in
a Commonwealth, as long as they are
ufed in their right kind ; the play-
makers worthy of honour for their art,
and players, men deferving both praife
and profit as long as they wax neither
covetous nor infolent. ('Never too Late'
[1590], viii., pp. 131-133.)

ENGLISH PLAYER.

Roberto [=Robert Greene] wondering to hear fuch good words, for that
this golden age affords few that efteem
of virtue ; returned him thankful gratu-
lations, and (urged by neceffity) uttered
his prefent grief, befeeching his advice
how he might be employed. Why,
eafily, quoth he, and greatly to your
benefit ; for men of my profeffion get
by fcholars their whole living. What
is your profeffion ? faid Roberto. Truly,
fir, faid he, I am a Player. A player,
quoth Roberto, I took you rather for a
gentleman of great living, for if by outward habit men fhould be cenfured

[= judged], I tell you, you would be taken for a fubftantial man. So am I where I dwell (quoth the Player), reputed able at my proper coft to build a windmill. What though the world once went hard with me, when I was fain to carry my playing fardle [= bundle] a-footback. *Tempora mutantur*, I know you know the meaning of it better than I, but I thus conftrue it. It is otherwife now ; for my very fhare in playing apparell will not be fold for two hundred pounds. Truly, faid Roberto, it is ftrange, that you fhould fo profper in that vain practice, for that it feems to me your voice is nothing gracious. Nay, then, faid the Player, I miflike your judgment : why, I am as famous for Delphrigus and the king of Fairies as ever was any of my time. The twelve labours of Hercules have I terribly thundered on the ftage and placed three fcenes of the devil on the highway to heaven. Have ye fo ? (faid Roberto), then I pray you pardon me. Nay, more (quoth the Player), I can ferve to make a pretty fpeech, for I was a country Author, paffing at a moral, for it was I that penned the moral of man's wit, the Dialogue of Dives, and for seven years' space was absolute interpreter of the puppets. But now my almanac is out of date.

> The people make no estimation
> Of Morals teaching education.

Was not this pretty for a plain rhyme extempore? If ye will ye shall have more. (' Groat's-worth of Wit' [1592], xii., pp. 130-132.)

GOOD ADVICES.

The Farewell of a Friend.

1. Let God's worship be thy morning's work, and His wisdom the direction of thy day's labour.

2. Rise not without thanks, nor sleep not without repentance.

3. Choose but a few friends, and try those ; for the flatterer speaks fairest.

4. If thy wife be wise, make her thy secretary, else lock thy thoughts in thy heart, for women are seldom silent.

5. If she be fair, be not jealous ; for suspicion cures not women's follies.

6. If she be wife wrong her not : for if thou lovest others she will loath thee.

7. Let thy children's nurture be their richest portion ; for wisdom is more precious than wealth.

8. Be not proud amongst thy poor neighbours : for a poor man's hate is perilous.

9. Nor too familiar with great men ; for presumption wins disdain.

10. Neither be too prodigal in thy fare, nor die not indebted to thy belly, but enough is a feast.

11. Be not envious, lest thou fall in thine own thoughts.

12. Use patience, mirth and quiet ; for care is enemy to health.

(' Never too Late ' [1590], viii., pp. 168, 169.)

TO YOUNG MEN.

A young man led on by self-will (having the reins of liberty in his own hand) forseeth not the ruth of folly, but aimeth at present pleasures : for he gives himself up to delight, and thinketh everything good, honest, lawful, and virtuous, that fitteth for the content of his lascivious humour. He forseeth not that such as climb hastily fall suddenly ; that bees have stings as well as honey ; that vices have ill ends as well as sweet beginnings. And whereof grows this heedless life, but of self-conceit, thinking the good counsel of age is dotage ; that the advice of friends proceeds of envy, and not of love ; that when their fathers correct them for their faults, they hate them : whereas when the black ox hath trod on their feet and the crow's foot is seen in their eyes, then, touched with the feeling of their own folly, they sigh out, ' Had I wist !' when repentance cometh too late. Or like as wax is ready to receive every new form that is stamped into it, so is youth apt to admit of every vice that is objected unto it, and in young years wanton desires is chiefly predominate, especially the two ringleaders of all other mischiefs, namely, pride and whoredom. These are the Syrens that with their enchanting melodies draw them on to utter confusion. . . . [Therefore bethink. . . .] (' Repentance ' 1592], xii., pp. 157, 158.)

UNVENERABLE OLD AGE.

Thefe two patterns of unrighteouf-
nefs and mirrors of mifchief, had under
the pens of a dove covered the heart of
a kite, under their fheeps' fkins hidden
the bloody nature of a wolf; thinking
under the fhadow of their grey hairs to
cover the fubftance of their treacherous
minds; in a painted fheath to hide a
rufty blade; in a filver bell a leaden
clapper, and in their aged complexion
moft youthful concupifcence, hoping
their hoary hairs would keep them
without blame and their grey heads
without fufpicion. Indeed, age is a
crown of glory when it is adorned with
righteoufnefs, but the dregs of difhonour
when it is mingled with mifchief. For
honourable age confifteth not in the
term of years, nor is not meafured by
the date of a man's days, but godly
wifdom is the grey hair and an un-
defiled life is old age. The herb
Grace, the older it is the ranker fmell
it hath, the Sea-ftar is moft black being
old, the older the eagle is the more
crooked is her bill, and the more age

in wicked men the more unrighteous.
('Mirror of Modefty' [1584], iii., pp.
11, 12.)

APOPHTHEGMS AND APT SAYINGS.

It is vain to water the plant when
the root is dead. ('Morando,' iii., p.
54.)

I count liking without law no love
but luft. (*Ibid.*, p. 59.)

It is hard . . . to hide Vulcan's polt
foot with pulling on a ftraight fhoe.
(*Ibid.*, p. 60.)

He who yieldeth himfelf as a flave to
love bindeth himfelf in fetters of gold,
and if his fuit have good fuccefs, yet he
leadeth his life in gliftering mifery.
(*Ibid.*, p. 86.)

A word miftaken is half a challenge.
(*Ibid.*, p. 127.)

When the boar layeth down his
briftles then he meaneth to ftrike.
('Anatomy of Fortune,' iii., p. 183.)

The Painter cafteth his faireft colour
over the fouleft board. (*Ibid.*)

Fortune, yea, fortune, in favouring

me hath made me moſt infortunate. (*Ibid.*, p. 184.)

The lapwing [= peewit] cries fartheſt off from her neſt. ('Tritameron,' iii., p. 78.) [*Cf.* 'Meaſure for Meaſure,' I., iv., 32 ; 'Comedy of Errors,' IV., ii., 27.—G.]

[Follow] the example of the induſtrious and painful [= painſtaking] bee, which draweth honey out of flowers and hurteth not the fruit. (*Ibid.*, p. 153.) [So George Herbert finely :

'Rain, do not hurt my flowers, but gently spend
  Your honey-drops ; press not to smell them, bee.'—G.]

Rather love by ear than like by the eye. ('Mirror,' iii., p. 10.)

A ſure truth . . . needs no ſubtle gloſs. (*Ibid.*, p. 60.)

['Tis] to pull on Hercules' hoſe on a child's foot. (*Ibid.*, p. 68.)

'Tis an ill flaw [= ſtorm-wind] that bringeth up no wreck . . . and a bad wind that breedeth no man's profit. (*Ibid.*, p. 84.)

I think of lovers as Diogenes did of dancers, who, being aſked how he liked

them, anfwered, The better the worfe.
(*Ibid.*, p. 88.) [So Dr. Johnfon of an
intricate and difficult mufical compofi-
tion, ' I wifh it had been fo difficult as
to be impoffible.'—G.]

Finding, with Scipio, that he was
never lefs alone than when he was
alone. (*Ibid.*, p. 114.) [Made im-
mortal by *Childe Harold.*—G.]

Wilt thou fhrink for an April fhower ?
(*Ibid.*, p. 214.)

That which is eafily begun is not
always lightly ended. ('Debate,' iv.,
p. 198.)

Stars are to be looked at with the
eye, not reached at with the hand.
('Doraftus,' iv., p. 285.)

My white hairs are bloffoms for the
grave. (*Ibid.*, p. 271.) [Percy, in his
'Reliques' (ii., 177, ed. 1812), quotes
the following as part of an old fong on
the ftory of the Beggar of Bethnal
Green :

'The reverend lockes in comelye curles did
    wave,
And on his aged temples grewe *the blossoms
    of the grave.*'

Qy. the ' old faying ' by Greene ?—G.]

The four bud will never be the sweet blossom.   ('Card,' iv., p. 15.)

She that is won with a word will be lost with a wind.   (*Ibid.*, p. 56.)

Make a virtue of necessity.   (*Ibid.*, p. 60.)

Too much familiarity breeds contempt.   (*Ibid.*, p. 102.)

I dare not infer comparisons because they be odious.   (*Ibid.*, p. 149.)

Adultery shall fly in the air, and thy known virtues shall lie hid in the earth. ('Doraftus,' iv., p. 250.)   [Ennobled by Shakespeare into :

'The evil that men do lives after them,
The good is oft interrèd with their bones.'
('Julius Cæsar,' II., x., 2.)—G.]

They went like shadows, not men. (*Ibid.*, p. 262.)

Falls come not by sitting low, but by climbing too high.   (*Ibid.*, p. 285.)

A woman's fault, to spurn at that with her foot which she greedily catcheth at with her hand.   (*Ibid.*, p. 285.)

Necessity hath no law.   (*Ibid.*, p. 294.)

Like the porcupine, who, coveting to strike others with her pens, leaveth herfelf void of any defence. ('Plancto-machia,' v., p. 97.) [Even Shakefpeare believed in the 'pen-propelling porcu-pine,' *e.g.*, 'Henry VI.,' III., i., 363 ; 'Troilus,' II., i., 27.—G.]

Is thy fancy fo fickle as every face muft be viewed with affection ? Fond man, think this, that the poor man maketh as great account of his wife as the greateft monarch in the world doth of an emprefs ; that honefty harbours as foon in a cottage as in the Court. ('Penelope's Web,' v., p. 205.)

For all the crack my penny may be good filver. (*Ibid.*, p. 233.)

Fair promifes and fmall performance. ('Planctomachia,' v., p. 43.)

More foon come than welcome. (*Ibid.*, p. 77.)

Cats' half-waking winks are but trains [= fnares] to entrap the moufe. (*Ibid.*, p. 84.)

Better to truft an open enemy than a reconciled friend. (*Ibid.*, p. 90.)

The longeft fummer's day hath his evening. (*Ibid.*, p. 129.)

Nothing is evil that is neceffary. ('Penelope's Web,' v., p. 178.) [= all that is is right.—G.]

My profeffion is your trade. ('Menaphon,' vi., p. 120.)

How happy are we that eat to live
and live not to eat. ('Perimedes,' vii.,
p. 21.)

The fox had his fkin pulled over his
ears for prying into the lion's den : poor
men fhould look no higher than their
feet, left in ftaring at ftars they ftumble.
(*Ibid.*, p. 22.)

Venus, I grant, hath a wrinkle in her
brow, but two dimples in her cheeks.
(*Ibid.*, p. 69.)

Words have wings, and once let flip
can never be recalled. ('Royal Ex-
change,' vii., p. 232.)

Poorly content is better than richly
covetous. ('Perimedes,' vii., p. 60.)

A woman, and therefore to be won.
(*Ibid.*, p. 68.)

Love beginneth in gold and endeth
in beggary. ('Never too Late,' viii.,
p. 36.)

Such as marry but to a fair face tie
themfelves oft to a foul bargain. (*Ibid.*)

Faireft bloffoms are fooneft nipped
with froft. (*Ibid.*, p. 71.)

A friend to [whom] to reveal is a
medicine to relieve. (*Ibid.*, p. 85.)

A woman's heart and her tongue are not relatives. (*Ibid.*, p. 90.)

She found that all his corn was on the floor. (*Ibid.*, p. 102.)

To bed with the bee and up with the lark. (*Ibid.*, p. 124.)

The crow thinks her fowls the faireft. (*Ibid.*, p. 186.) [A play on 'foul.']

In many words lieth miftruft, and in painted fpeech deceit is often covered. ('Metamorphofis,' ix., 73.)

May not a woman look but fhe muft love ? (*Ibid.*, p. 83.)

Making a woman's refiftance. (*Ibid.*, p. 104.)

Truft not him that fmiles. ('Mourning Garment' [1590], ix., p. 138. [*Cf.* 'Hamlet,' i., 5 : 'Smile, and fmile, and be a villain.'—G.]

Hunger needs no fauce and thirft turns water into wine. (*Ibid.*, p. 145.)

Ah, father, had I reverenced my God as I honoured my goddefs ! (*Ibid.*, p. 207.)—G. [*Cf.* 'Henry VIII.,' iii., 2.]

Parrots fpeak not what they think. ('Farewell,' p. 246.)

Bring not contempt to fuch a royal dignity by too much familiarity. (*Ibid.*, p. 258.)

The ploughman hath more eafe than a king. (*Ibid.*, p. 277.)

We have as much health with feeding on the brown loaf as a prince hath with all his delicates, and I fteal more fweet naps in the chimney corner in a week than God fave his majefty! (*Ibid.*)

You may fmell their pride by their perfumes. (*Ibid.*, p. 285.)

Love filleth not the hand with pelf, but the eye with pleafure. (*Ibid.*, p. 300.)

It is not riches to have much, but to defire little. (*Ibid.*, p. 309.)

Drink me as dry as a fieve. ('Life and Death of Ned Browne,' xi., p. 30.)

Envy creepeth not fo low as cottages. ('Philomela,' xi., p. 176.)

Acquaint not thyfelf with many, left thou fall into the hands of flatterers. (*Ibid.*)

Courteous to all, but converfe with few. (*Ibid.*)

Truth is the daughter of Time. (*Ibid.*, p. 189.)

Time hatcheth truth. (*Ibid.*, p. 197.)

The tailor fews with hot needle and burnt thread. (*Ibid.*, p. 238.)

Will is above fkill. ('Orpharion,' xii., p. 5.)

Pierced by Achilles' lance muſt be healed by his ſpear. (*Ibid.,* p. 9.)

Buy ſmoke with many perils and dangers. (*Ibid.,* p. 10.)

Reap many kiſſes and little love. (*Ibid.,* p. 17.)

Ay, quench fire with flax. (*Ibid.,* p. 39.)

He never played in jeſt. (*Ibid.,* p. 58.)

King's words may not offend. (*Ibid.,* p. 72.)

Like the pace of a crab, backward. (*Ibid.,* p. 75.)

We are only overcome, not vanquiſhed. (*Ibid.,* p. 88.)

Once get into the bone, it will ſtep into the fleſh. ('Repentance,' xii., p. 159.)

Blamed, but never aſhamed. ('Viſion,' xii., p. 248.)

Aſk counſel of your pillow. (*Ibid.,* p. 265.)

The biggeſt limbs have not the ſtouteſt hearts (l. 1091).

Empty veſſels have the loudeſt ſounds,
And cowards prattle more than men of worth (ll. 1101, 1102).

('The Pinner of Wakefield' [1599].)

O, Sir, I love the fruit that tr eafon brings,
But thofe that are the traitors, them I
 hate.
         (' Selinus,' ll. 1259, 1260.)
' White-wing'd victory fits on our fwords '
                    (l. 1585).

           ' Caft to compafs it
Without delay, or long procraftination ;
It argueth an unmaturèd wit
When all is ready for fo ftrong invafion
To draw out time ; an unlook'd-for
 mutation
May foon prevent us if we do delay :
Quick fpeed is good, where wifdom
 leads the way.
          (*Ibid.*, ll. 307-313.)
But friends are men, and love can baffle
 lords :
The earl both woos and courts her for
 himfelf.
        (' Friar Bacon,' ll. 639, 640).
Pity me, though I be a farmer's fon,
And meafure not my riches, but my love.
          (*Ibid.*, ll. 764, 765.)
        Love's foolifh looks
Think footfteps miles and minutes to be
 hours.
         (*Ibid.*, ll. 1155, 1156.)

Old folk are twice children. ('Mam-illia,' ii., p. 50.) [Robert Ferguſſon, precurſor of Robert Burns, felicitouſly puts it in his 'Farmer's Ingle '—proto-type of the 'Cottar's Saturday Night':

'The mind's aye cradled when the grave is
    near.'—G.]

They feek others where they have been hid themſelves. (*Ibid.*, p. 16.)

He that cannot diſſemble cannot live. (*Ibid.*, p. 19.)

A young faint, an old devil. (*Ibia.*, p. 25.) [A long-lived lie, ſlander and ſneer combined.—G.]

One forecaſt is worth two after. (*Ibid.*, p. 26.)

Killed her with kindneſs. (*Ibid.*)

Two might beſt keep counſel where one was away. (*Ibid.*, p. 30.)

It is a foul bird that defiles its own neſt. (*Ibid.*, p. 31.) [But it is only its own neſt that it can well defile.—G.]

The beſt clerks are not ever the wiſeſt men. (*Ibid.*, p. 34.)

The fox will eat no grapes. (*Ibid.*, p. 52.)

Love makes all men orators. (*Ibid.*, p. 57.)

One tale is always good until another is told. (*Ibid.*, p. 222.)

Pull hair from a bald man's head. (*Ibid.*, p. 225.)

ALLITERATION.

Reject not him fo rigoroufly which refpecteth you fo reverently; loath him not fo hatefully which loveth you fo heartily, nor repay not his dutiful amity with fuch deadly enmity. ('Card of Fancy' [1587], iv., p. 113.)

To hope ftill, I fee is but to heap woe upon wretchedness, and care upon calamity. Yet, madam, thus much I will fay, that Dido, Queen of Carthage, loved Æneas, a banifhed exile and a ftraggling ftranger. Euphinia, daughter to the King of Corinth, and heir-apparent to his crown, who for her feature [= perfon] was famous through-out all the Eaft countries, vouchfafed to apply a fovereign plafter to the furious paffions of Acharifto, her father's bond-man. The Duchefs of Malfy chofe for her hufband her fervant Ulrico; and

Venus, who for furpaffing beauty was canonized for a goddefs, difdained not the love of limping Vulcan. They, madam, refpected the men, and not their money; their wills, and not their wealth; their love, not their livings; their conftancy, not their coin; their perfon, not their parentage; and the inward virtue, not the outward value. But you are fo addicted to the opinion of Danae, that unlefs Jupiter himfelf be fhrouded in your lap, under the fhape of a fhower of gold, he fhall have the repulfe for all his deity. (*Ibid.*, p. 119.)

A NOBLE HEAD—FRIAR BACON.

Vandermaft. Lordly thou lookeft, as if that thou wert learn'd;
  Thy countenance, as if fcience held her feat
  Between the circled arches of thy brows.
  ('Friar Bacon,' vol. xiii., ll. 1297-99.)

FRIAR BACON.

Seeing you come as friends unto the friar,
Refolve you doctors, Bacon can by books
Make ftorming Boreas thunder from his
    cave,
And dim fair Luna to a dark eclipfe.
The great arch-ruler, potentate of Hell,
Trembles, when Bacon bids him, or his
    fiends,
Bow to the force of his pentageron.
What Art can work, the frolic friar
    knows ;
And therefore will I turn my magic
    books,
And ftrain out necromancy to the deep :
I have contriv'd and fram'd a head of
    brafs
(I made Belcephon hammer out the
    ftuff),
And that by Art fhall read philofophy,
And I will ftrengthen England by my
    fkill,
That if ten Cæsars lived and reign'd in
    Rome,
With all the legions Europe doth contain,
They fhould not touch a grafs of Englifh
    ground :

The work that Ninus rear'd at Babylon,
The brazen walls fram'd by Semiramis,
Carv'd out like to the portal of the fun ;
Shall not be fuch as rings the Englifh
   ftrand,
From Dover to the market-place of Rye.
     ('Friar Bacon,' xiii., pp. 16, 17.)

BEAUTY—A SONG.

Beauty, alas ! where waft thou born,
Thus to hold thyfelf in fcorn ?
When as Beauty kifs'd to woo thee,
Thou by Beauty doft undo me,
   Heigho, defpife me not.
I and thou, in footh are one,
Faireft thou, ay fairer none ;
Wanton thou, and wilt thou wanton,
Yield a cruel heart to pant on ?
Do me right, and do me reafon,
Cruelty is curfèd treafon :
   Heigho, I love ; heigho, I love !
   Heigho ; and yet he eyes me not.
('A Looking-glafs for London and Eng-
   land' [1594], xiv., 74, 75.)

BOHEMIA—SHAKESPEARE ILLUSTRATION.

It ſo happened that Egiſtus, King of Sicily, who in his youth had been brought up with Pandoſto, deſirous to ſhow that neither tract of time, nor diſtance of place, could diminiſh their former friend-ſhip, provided a navy of ſhips and *ſailed into Bohemia* to viſit his old friend and companion . . . ('Hiſtory of Doraſtus and Fawnia' [1588], iv., p. 235). [Every-one knows Shakeſpeare's kindred ſlip in 'Winter's Tale'; but this 19th century could ſhow juſt as great geographical blunders, *e.g.*, about Africa and India, etc., etc. *Cf.* alſo note in Works, vol. v., pp. 304, 305, as bearing on Shake-ſpeare's alleged 'ſmall Latin and leſs Greek.'—G.]

CHASTITY—AN ODE.

What is love once diſgracèd ?
But a wanton thought ill placèd,
Which doth blemiſh whom it paineth,
And diſhonours whom it deigneth.

Seen in higher powers moft,
Though fome fools do fondly boaft
That whofo is high of kin
Sanctifies his lover's fin.
Jove could not hide Io's fcape,
Nor conceal Califto's rape.
Both did fault, and both were fam*è*d,
Light of loves whom luft had fham*è*d.
Let not women truft to men,
They can flatter now and then.
And tell them many wanton tales,
Which do breed their after bales.
Sin in kings is fin we fee,
And greater fin, 'caufe great of 'gree.
Majus peccatum, this I read,
If he be high that doth the deed.
Mars for all his deity
Could not Venus dignify.
But Vulcan trapp'd her, and her blame,
Was punifhed with an open fhame.
All the gods laugh'd them to fcorn,
For dubbing Vulcan with the horn.
Whereon may a woman boaft,
If her chaftity be loft ?
Shame awaiteth upon her face,
Blufhing cheeks and foul difgrace :
Report will blab, this is fhe
That with her lufts wins infamy.
If lufting love be fo difgrac'd,

Die before you live unchaste.
For better die with honeft fame,
Than lead a wanton life with fhame !
('Philomela' [1592], xi., pp. 178, 179.)

COMEDY.*

*Enter the Clown and his crew of Ruffians,
to go to drink.*

Firft Ruffian. Come on, Smith, thou
fhalt be one of the crew, becaufe thou
knoweft where the beft ale in the town is.

Adam [the blackfmith's man]. Come
on, in faith, my colts : I have left my
Mafter ftriking of a heat, and ftole away,
becaufe I would keep you company.

Clown. Why, what, fhall we have this
paltry Smith with us ?

Adam. Paltry Smith ? Why, you in-
carnative knave, what are you that you
fpeak petty treafon againft the fmith's
trade ?

Clown. Why, flave, I am a gentleman
of Niniveh ?

* These are examples of Green's remarkable
comic vein.—G.

Adam. A gentleman? Good Sir, I remember you well, and all your progenitors: your father bare office in our town; an honeſt man he was, and in great diſcredit in the pariſh, for they beſtowed two ſquire's livings on him; the one was on working-days, and then he kept the town ſtage, and on holidays they made him the Sexton's man, for he whipped dogs out of the church. Alas, Sir, your father,—why, Sir, methinks I ſee the gentleman ſtill: a proper youth he was, faith, aged ſome forty and ten; his beard rat's colour, half black, half white; his noſe was in the higheſt degree of noſes, it was noſe *autem glorificam,* ſo ſet with rubies that after his death it ſhould have been nailed up in Copperſmith's Hall for a monument: well, Sir, I was beholding to your good father, for he was the firſt man that ever inſtructed me in the myſtery of a pot of ale.

Second Ruffian. Well ſaid, Smith; that croſſed him over the thumbs.

Clown. Villain, were it not that we go to be merry, my rapier ſhould preſently quit thy opprobrious terms.

Adam. O, Peter, Peter, put up thy

ſword, I prithee heartily, into thy ſcab-
bard, hold in your rapier ; for though I
have not a long reacher, I have a ſhort
hitter.—Nay then, gentlemen, ſtay me,
for my choler begins to riſe againſt him ;
for mark the words, 'a paltry ſmith.'
Oh, horrible ſentence : thou haſt in theſe
words, I will ſtand to it, libelled againſt
all the ſound horſes, whole horſes, ſore
horſes, courſers, curtalls, jades, cuts,
hackneys, and mares ; whereupon, my
friend, in their defence, I give thee this
curſe,—thou ſhalt not be worth a horſe
of thine own this ſeven year.

Clown. Ay, prithee ſmith, is your
occupation ſo excellent ?

Adam. 'A paltry ſmith'? Why, I'll
ſtand to it, a ſmith is lord of the four
elements ; for our iron is made of the
earth, our bellows blow out air, our floor
holds fire, and our forge water. Nay,
Sir, we read in the Chronicles that there
was a god of our occupation.

Clown. Ay, but he was a cuckold.

Adam. That was the reaſon, Sir, he
called your father couſin. 'Paltry
ſmith'? why, in this one word thou haſt
defaced their worſhipful occupation.

Clown. As how ?

Adam. Marry, Sir, I will ſtand to it, that a ſmith in his kind is a phyſician, a ſurgeon, and a barber. For let a horſe take a cold, or be troubled with the botts, and we ſtraight give him a potion or a purgation, in ſuch phyſical manner that he mends ſtraight : if he have outward diſeaſes, as the ſpavin, ſplent, ring-bone, wind-gall, or *farcin*, or, Sir, a galled back, we let him blood and clap a plaſter to him with a peſti- lence, that mends him with a very vengeance : now, if his mane grow out of order, and he have any rebellious hairs, we ſtraight to our ſhears and trim him with what cut it pleaſe us, pick his ears, and make him neat. Marry, in- deed, Sir, we are ſlovens for one thing ; we never uſe any muſk-balls to waſh him with, and the reaſon, Sir, becauſe he can woe* without kiſſing.

Clown. Well, ſirrha, leave off theſe praiſes of a ſmith, and bring us to the beſt ale in the town.

Adam. Now, Sir, I have a feat above all the ſmiths in Niniveh ; for, Sir, I am a philoſopher that can diſpute of the nature of ale ; for mark you, Sir, a pot

* = play on ' woo.'—G.

of ale confifts of four parts,—Imprimis the ale, the toaft, the ginger, and the nutmeg.

Clown. Excellent.

Adam. The ale is a reftorative, bread is a binder; mark you, Sir, two excellent points in phyfic : the ginger, oh, 'ware of that : the philofophers have written of the nature of ginger, 'tis expulfitive in two degrees : you fhall hear the fentence of Galen :

    ' *It will make a man belch, cough, and —,*
      And is a great comfort to the heart ' :

a proper pofie, I promife you : but now to the noble virtue of nutmeg : it is, saith one ballad, (I think an Englifh Roman was the author,) an underlayer to the brains, for when the ale gives a buffet to the head, oh, the nutmeg that keeps him for a while in temper. Thus you fee the defcription of the virtue of a pot of ale. Now, Sir, to put my phyfical precepts in practice, follow me : but afore I ftep any further——

Clown. What's the matter now ?

Adam. Why, feeing I have provided the ale, who is the purveyor for the wenches ? for, mafters, take this of me,

a cup of ale without a wench, why,
alas! 'tis like an egg without falt, or a
red herring without muftard!

Clown. Lead us to the ale: we'll have
wenches enough, I warrant thee.

[*Exeunt.*

('A Looking-glafs for London and England' [1594], xiv., 15-20.)

AN ONWARD SCENE.

Enters Adam, the Clown.

Adam. This way he is, and here will
I fpeak with him.

Lord. Fellow, whither preffeth thou?

Adam. I prefs nobody, Sir; I am
going to fpeak with a friend of mine.

Lord. Why, flave, there is none but
the king and his viceroys.

Adam. The king? Marry, Sir, he is
the man I would fpeak withal.

Lord. Why, calleft him a friend of
thine?

Adam. Ay, marry do I, Sir; for if he
be not my friend, I'll make him my
friend ere he and I pafs.

Lord. Away, vaffal, begone, thou fpeak unto the king!

Adam. Ay, marry, will I, Sir; and if he were a king of velvet, I will talk to him.

Rafni (the king). What's the matter there? what noife is that?

Adam. A boon, my liege! a boon, my liege!

Rafni. What is it that great Rafni will not grant,

This day, unto the meaneft of his land,

In honour of his beauteous Alvida?

Come hither, fwain; what is it that thou craveft?

Adam. Faith, Sir, nothing but to fpeak a few fentences to your worfhip.

Rafni. Say, what is it?

Adam. I am fure, Sir, you have heard of the fpirits that walk in the city here.

Rafni. Ay, what of that?

Adam. Truly, Sir, I have an oration to tell you of one of them; and this it is.

Alvida (queen). Why goeft not forward with thy tale?

Adam. Faith, miftrefs, I feel an imperfection in my voice, a difeafe that often troubles me; but, alas! eafily mended; a cup of ale or a cup of wine will ferve the turn.

Alvida. Fill him a bowl, and let him want no drink.

Adam. Oh, what a precious word was that, 'And let him want no drink.' [*Drink given to Adam.*] Well, Sir, now I'll tell you forth my tale : Sir, as I was coming alongft the port-royal of Niniveh, there appeared to me a great devil, and as hard-favoured a devil as ever I faw ; nay, Sir, he was a cuckoldy devil, for he had horns on his head. This devil, mark you now, preffeth upon me, and, Sir, indeed, I charged him with my pikeftaff ; but when that would not ferve, I came upon him with *Spiritus fanctus,*—why, it had been able to have put Lucifer out of his wits : when I faw my charm would not ferve, I was in fuch a perplexity that fix pennyworth of juniper would not have made the place fweet again.

Alvida. Why, fellow, wert thou fo afraid ?

Adam. Oh, miftrefs, had you been there and feen, his very fight had made you fhift a clean fmock, I promife you ; though I were a man, and counted a tall fellow, yet my laundrefs called me flovenly knave the next day.

E

Rafni. A pleafant flave.—Forward, Sir, on with thy tale.

Adam. Faith, Sir, but I remember a word that my miftrefs, your bed-fellow, fpoke.

Rafni. What was that, fellow?

Adam. Oh, Sir, a word of comfort, a precious word—'And let him want no drink.'

Rafni. Her word is law; and thou fhalt want no drink.

[*Drink given to Adam.*

Adam. Then, Sir, this devil came upon me, and would not be perfuaded, but he would needs carry me to hell. I proffered him a cup of ale, thinking, becaufe he came out of fo hot a place, that he was thirfty; but the devil was not dry, and therefore the more forry was I. Well, there was no remedy, but I muft with him to hell: and at laft I caft mine eye afide; if you knew what I fpied you would laugh, Sir. I looked from top to toe, and he had no cloven feet. Then I ruffled up my hair, and fet my cap on the one fide; and, Sir, grew to be a Juftice of Peace to the devil. At laft, in a great fume, as I am very choleric, and fometime fo hot in my fuſtian fumes, that no man can abide within twenty yards of me, I ſtart up, and ſo bombaſted the devil that, Sir, he cried out and ran away.

    Alvida. This pleaſant knave hath
        made me laugh my fill :
Raſni, now Alvida begins her quaff,
And drinks a full carouſe unto her king.
    Raſni. Ay, pledge, my love, as hearty
        as great Jove
Drunk when his Juno heav'd a bowl to
        him.—
Frolic, my lords, let all the ſtandards
        walk ;
Ply it till every man hath ta'en his load.—
How now, ſirrha, what cheer? we have
        no words of you.
    Adam. Truly, Sir, I was in a brown ſtudy about my miſtreſs.
    Alvida. About me ? for what ?
    Adam. Truly, miſtreſs, to think what a golden ſentence you did ſpeak : all the philoſophers in the world could not have ſaid more ;—'What, come, let him want no drink.' Oh, wiſe ſpeech !
    Alvida. Villains, why ſkink you not
        unto this fellow ?
He makes me blyth and merry in my
        thoughts :

Heard you not that the king hath given
    command,
That all be drunk this day within his
    Court,
In quaffing to the health of Alvida ?
                    [*Drink given to Adam.*
                    (*Ibid.*, pp. 90-94.)

FINAL SCENE.

*Enters Adam folus, with a bottle of beer
    in one flop* [= loofe troufers] *and a
    great piece of beef in another.*

Adam. Well, goodman Jonah, I would
you had never come from Jewry to this
country ; you have made me look like a
lean rib of roaft beef, or like the picture
of Lent painted upon a red herring's
cob. Alas, mafters, we are commanded
by the proclamation to faft and pray :
by my troth, I could prettily fo, fo away
with praying ; but for fafting, why 'tis
fo contrary to my nature, that I had rather
fuffer a fhort hanging than a long
fafting. Mark me, the words be thefe,
' Thou fhalt take no manner of food for
fo many days.' I had as lieve he fhould
have faid, ' Thou fhalt hang thyfelf for
fo many days.' And yet, in faith, I

need not find fault with the proclamation, for I have a buttery and a pantry,
and a kitchen about me ; for proof *Ecce
fignum !* This right flop is my pantry ;
behold a manchet [*Draws it out*]; this
place is my kitchen, for lo ! a piece of
beef [*Draws it out*],—Oh, let me repeat
that fweet word again : for lo ! a piece
of beef ! This is my buttery, for fee,
fee, my friends, to my great joy, a bottle
of beer [*Draws it out*]. Thus, alas ! I
make fhift to wear out this fafting ; I
drive away the time. But there go
fearchers about to feek if any man
breaks the king's commands. Oh, here
they be ; in with your victuals, Adam.
[*Puts them back into his flops.*

Enter two Searchers.

Firft Searcher. How duly the men of
Niniveh keep the proclamation ; how
are they armed to repentance ! We
have fearched through the whole city,
and have not as yet found one that
breaks the faft.

Second Searcher. The fign of the more
grace:—but ftay, here fits one, methinks,
at his prayers ; let us fee who it is.

Firft Searcher. 'Tis Adam, the fmith's man.—How now, Adam?

Adam. Trouble me not; ' Thou fhalt take no manner of food, but faft and pray.'

Firft Searcher. How devoutly he fits at his orifons; but ftay, methinks, I feel a fmell of fome meat or bread about him.

Second Searcher. So thinks me too.— You, firrha, what victuals have you about you?

Adam. Victuals! O horrible blaf- phemy! Hinder me not of my prayer, nor drive me not into a choler. Victuals! why heardeft thou not the fentence, ' Thou fhalt take no food, but faft and pray'?

Second Searcher. Truth, fo it fhould be; but, methinks, I fmell meat about thee.

Adam. About me, my friends? Thefe words are actions in the cafe. About me? No, no; hang thofe gluttons that cannot faft and pray.

Firft Searcher. Well, for all your words, we muft fearch you.

Adam. Search me! Take heed what you do; my hofe are my caftles; 'tis burglary if you break ope a flop: no officer muſt lift up an iron hatch ; take heed, my ſlops are iron.

[*They ſearch Adam.*

Second Searcher. Oh, villain, ſee how he hath gotten victuals, bread, beef, and beer, where the king commanded upon pain of death none ſhould eat for ſo many days ; no, not the ſucking in-fant.

Adam. Alas, ſir, this is nothing but a *modicum non nocet ut medicus daret ;* why, Sir, a bit to comfort my ſtomach.

Firſt Searcher. Villain, thou ſhalt be hanged for it.

Adam. Theſe are your words, ‘ I ſhall be hanged for it ;’ but firſt anſwer me to this queſtion, how many days have we to faſt ſtill ?

Second Searcher. Five days.

Adam. Five days : a long time : then I muſt be hanged ?

Firſt Searcher. Ay, marry, Sir, muſt thou.

Adam. I am your man, I am for you, Sir ; for I had rather be hanged than bide ſo long a faſt. What, five days ? Come, I’ll untruſs. Is your halter and the gallows, the ladder, and all ſuch furniture in readineſs ?

Firſt Searcher. I warrant thee ſhalt want none of theſe.

Adam. But, hear you, muſt I be hanged?

Firſt Searcher. Ay, marry.

Adam. And for eating of meat. Then, friends, know ye by theſe preſents, I will eat up all my meat, and drink up all my drink ; for it ſhall never be ſaid I was hanged with an empty ſtomach.

Firſt Searcher. Come away, knave ; wilt thou ſtand feeding now?

Adam. If you be ſo haſty, hang your-ſelf an hour, while I come to you, for ſurely I will eat up my meat.

Second Searcher. Come, let's draw him away perforce.

Adam. You ſay there is five days yet to faſt, theſe are your words.

Second Searcher. Ay, Sir.

Adam. I am for you : come, let's away, and yet let me be put in the Chronicles.   [*Exeunt.*

(*Ibid.,* pp. 105-109.)

A CONTENTED MIND.

Sweet are the thoughts that favour of
    content ;
    The quiet mind is richer than a
    crown ;
Sweet are the nights in carelefs flumber
    fpent ;
    The poor eftate fcorns Fortune's
    angry frown :
Such fweet content, fuch minds, fuch
    fleep, fuch blifs,
Beggars enjoy, when princes oft do
    mifs.
The homely houfe that harbours quiet
    reft ;
    The cottage that affords no pride nor
    care ;
The mean that 'grees with country
    mufic beft ;
    The fweet comfort of mirth and
    modeft* fare ;

* The original has 'music's fare.' The word
had been caught from the preceding verse.
My venerable friend, W. J. Linton, in his
'Rare Poems,' reads as above, and it is inevitably accepted.—G.

Obfcurèd life fets down a type of blifs,
A mind content both crown and kingdom is.
('Farewell to Folly' [1591], ix., pp.
279, 280.)

CONTENT.

Barmeniſſa's Seng.

The cottage feated in the hollow dale,
That Fortune never fears becaufe fo low;
The quiet mind that Want doth fet to
fale,
Sleeps fafe, when prince's feats do over-
throw;
  Want fmiles fecure when princely
  thoughts do feel
  That Fear and Danger treads upon
  their heel.

Blefs Fortune thou whofe frown hath
  wrought thy good;
Bid farewell to the crown that ends thy
  care;

The happy fates thy forrows have with-
    ftood
By 'fygning want and poverty thy fhare ;
    For now content (fond Fortune to
    defpite)
    With patience 'lows* thee quiet and
    delight.
('Penelope's Web' [1587], v., p. 180.)

A COUNTRY BEAUTY.

Edward [*Prince of Wales*]. I tell thee,
    Lacy, that her fparkling eyes
Do lighten forth fweet Love's alluring
    fire :
And in her treffes fhe doth fold the
    looks
Of fuch as gaze upon her golden hair :
Her bafhful white, mixed with the
    morning's red,
Luna doth boaft upon her lovely cheeks:
Her front is Beauty's table, where fhe
    paints
The glories of her gorgeous excellence :
Her teeth are fhelves of precious mar-
    garites,

             * *allows.*

Richly enclofed with ruddy coral cliffs.
    'Tufh, Lacy, fhe is beauty's overmatch
If thou furveyeft her curious imagery.
    Lacy [*Earl of Lincoln*]. I grant, my
        lord, the damfel is as fair
As fimple Suffolk's homely towns can
    yield ;
But in the court be quainter dames than
    fhe ;
Whofe faces are enrich'd with honour's
    taint,*
Whofe beauties ftand upon the ftage of
    Fame,
And vaunt their trophies in the courts
    of Love.
    Edward. Ah, Ned, but hadft thou
        watch'd her as myfelf,
And feen the fecret beauties of the
    maid,
Their courtly coynefs were but foolery,
    Ermfbie. Why, how watch'd you her,
        my lord ?
    Edward. When as fhe fwept like Venus
        through the houfe,
And in her fhape faft folded up my
    thoughts ;
Into the Milkhoufe went I with the
    maid,

* tint.

And there amongſt the cream-bowls ſhe
    did ſhine,
As Pallas 'mongſt her princely huſ-
    wifery;
She turned her ſmock over her lily
    arms,
And div'd them into milk to run her
    cheeſe;
But whiter than the milk her cryſtal
    ſkin,
Check'd with lines of azure, made her
    bluſh,
That Art or Nature durſt bring for
    compare :
Ermſbie, if thou hadſt ſeen, as I did note
    it well,
How beauty play'd the huſwife, how
    this girl
Like Lucrece, laid her fingers to the
    work,
Thou wouldſt with Tarquin hazard
    Rome and all
To win the lovely maid of Freſingfield.
('Friar Bacon' [1594], xiii., pp. 9-11.)

CRADLE SONG.

Weep not, my wanton, fmile upon my
    knee ;
When thou art old there's grief enough
    for thee.
    Mother's wag, pretty boy,
    Father's forrow, father's joy ;
    When thy father firft did fee
    Such a boy by him and me,
    He was glad, I was woe ;
    Fortune changed made him fo ;
    When he left his pretty boy,
    Laft his forrow, firft his joy.

Weep not, my wanton, fmile upon my
    knee ;
When thou art old there's grief enough
    for thee.
    Streaming tears that never ftint,
    Like pearl-drops from a flint,
    Fell by courfe from his eyes,
    That one another's place fupplies ;
    Thus he grieved in every part,
    Tears of blood fell from his heart,
    When he left his pretty boy,
    Father's forrow, father's joy.

Weep not, my wanton, ſmile upon my
    knee ;
When thou art old there's grief enough
    for thee.
    The wanton ſmiled, father wept,
    Mother cried, baby leapt ;
    More he crowed, more we cried,
    Nature could not ſorrow hide :
    He muſt go, he muſt kiſs
    Child and mother, baby bliſs ;*
    For he left hiſ pretty boy,
    Father's ſorrow, father's joy.

Weep not, my wanton, ſmile upon my
    knee ;
When thou art old there's grief enough
    for thee.
('Menaphon' [1589], vi., pp. 43, 44.)

CUPID.

Ida. . . . I heard a ſhepherd ſing,
That like a bee, Love hath a little ſting:
He lurks in flowers, he percheth on the
    trees ;
He on king's pillows bends his pretty
    knees :
        * *bless.*

The boy is blind, but when he will not
    ſpy
He hath a leaded foot, and wings to fly:
Beſhrew me yet, for all theſe ſtrange
    effects
If I would like the lad that ſo infects.
    ('James the Fourth,' xiii., p. 216.)

THE EAGLE AND THE FLY.

When tender ewes, brought home with
    evening ſun,
    Wend to their folds,
    And to their holds
The ſhepherds trudge when light of day
    is done ;
    Upon a tree
The Eagle,—Jove's fair bird,—did
    perch ;
    There reſteth he :
A little Fly his harbour* then did ſearch,
And did preſume, though others laughed
    thereat,
To perch whereas† the princely Eagle
    ſat.

    * *arbour* or *shelter-place.*   † *whereon.*

The Eagle frowned, and fhook her royal
　　　wings,
　　　And charged the Fly
　　　From thence to hie :
Afraid, in hafte, the little creature flings,
　　　Yet feeks again,
Fearful, to perch him by the Eagle's
　　　fide :
　　　With moody vein,
The fpeedy poft of Ganymede replied :
' Vaffal, avaunt, or with my wings you
　　　die :
Is't fit an Eagle feat him with a Fly ?'

The Fly craved pity ; ftill the Eagle
　　　frown'd :
　　　The filly Fly,
　　　Ready to die,
Difgraced, difplaced, fell grovelling to
　　　the ground :
　　　The Eagle faw,
And with a royal mind faid to the Fly,
　　　' Be not in awe,
I fcorn by me the meaneft creature die ;
Then feat thee here.' The joyful Fly
　　　upflings,
And fat fafe-fhadowed with the Eagle's
　　　wings.
(' Menaphon ' [1589], vi., pp. 59, 60.)

*AN EPISTLE DEDICATORY.**
(Complete.)

To the gentlemen readers, Health. Gentlemen, I dare not ftep awry from my wonted method, firft to appeal to your favourable courtefies, which ever I have found (however plaufible) yet fmothered with a mild filence. The fmall pamphlets that I have thruft forth how you have regarded them I know not, but that they have been badly re-warded with any ill terms I never found; which makes me the more bold to trouble you, and the more bound to reft yours every way, as ever I have done. I keep my old courfe, to palter up fome thing in profe, ufing mine old pofy ftill, *omne tulit punctum;* although lately two gentlemen poets made two mad-men of Rome beat it out of their paper bucklers; and had it in derifion, for that I could not make my verfes fet upon the ftage in tragical bufkins, every word filling the mouth like the faburden

* Greene's 'Epistles Dedicatory,' like Breton's and Spenser's, are all graciously and finely worded.—G.

of Bow-Bell ; daring God out of heaven
with that atheift Tamburlane, or blaf-
pheming with the mad prieft of the
fun : but let me rather openly pocket
up the afs at Diogenes' hand, than
wantonly fet out fuch impious inftances
of intolerable poetry. Such mad and
fcoffing poets, that have prophetical
fpirits, as bred of Merlin's race, if there
be any in England, that fet the end of
fcholarifm in an Englifh blank verfe, I
think either it is the humour of a novice
that tickles them with felf-love, or too
much frequenting the hot-houfe (to ufe
the German proverb) hath fweat out all
the greateft part of their wits, which
wafte *gradatim*, as the Italians fay, *poco
à poco*. If I fpeak darkly, gentlemen,
and offend with this digreffion, I crave
pardon, in that I but anfwer in print
what they have offered on the ftage.
But leaving thefe fantaftical fcholars, as
judging him that is not able to make
choice of his chaffer but a peddling
chapman, at laft to *Perymedes the Blackfmith*, who, fitting in his holiday fuit to
enter parley with his wife, fmugged up
in her beft apparel, I prefent to your
favours. If he pleafe I have my defire,

if he but pafs I fhall be glad. If neither,
I vow to make amends in my *Orpharion*,
which I promife to make you merry
with the next term : And thus refting
on your wonted courtefies, I bid you
farewell. Yours as ever he hath been,
—R. Greene. ('Perimedes the Blackfmith' [1588], vii., pp. 7-9.)

FANCY.

Lamilia's Song.

Fie, fie on blind Fancy !
It hinders youth's joy ;
Fair virgins, learn by me
To count Love a toy.

When Love learned firft the A B C of
    delight,
And knew no figures nor conceited
    phrafe ;
He fimply gave to due defert her right,
He led not lovers in dark winding ways ;
He plainly willed to love, or flatly
    anfwered no :
But now who lifts to prove, fhall find it
    nothing fo.

Fie, fie, then, on Fancy !
It hinders youth's joy ;
Fair virgins, learn by me
To count Love a toy.

For fince he learned to ufe the poet's
pen,
He learned likewife with fmoothing
words to feign ;
Witching chafte ears with trothlefs
tongues of men,
And wrongèd faith with falfehood and
difdain ;
He gives a promife now, anon he
fweareth no :
Who lifteth for to prove, fhall find his
changing fo.
Fie, fie, then, on Fancy !
It hinders youth's joy ;
Fair virgins, learn by me
To count Love a toy.

('The Groats'-worth of Wit bought
with a Million of Repentance' [1592],
xii., pp. 113, 114.)

OLD ENGLISH FLOWERS.

Ah, Mullidor, her face is like to a red and white daify growing in a green meadow, and thou like a bee, that comeſt and ſuckeſt honey from it, and carrieſt it home to the hive with a heave and ho : that is as much as to ſay, as with a head full of woes and a heart full of ſorrows and maladies. Be of good cheer, Mirimida laughs on thee, and thou knoweſt a woman's ſmile is as good to a lover as a ſunſhine day to a haymaker. She ſhews thee kind looks and caſts many a ſheep's eye at thee ; which ſignifies that ſhe counts thee a man worthy to jump a match with her ; nay, more, Mullidor, ſhe hath given thee a noſegay of flowers, wherein, as a top gallant for all the reſt, is ſet in roſemary for remembrance. Ah, Mullidor, cheer thyſelf, fear not. Love, and fortune favour luſty lads ; cowards are not friends to affection : therefore venture, for thou haſt won her ; elſe ſhe had not given thee this noſegay. ('Never too Late' [1590], viii., pp. 197, 198.)

Thereby I faw the Batchelors' Buttons, whofe virtue it is to make wanton maidens weep when they have worn it forty weeks under their aprons for a favour. Next them grew the diffembling daify, to warn fuch light of love wenches not to truft every fair promife that fuch amorous bachelors make them, but [that] fweet fmells breed bitter repentance. Hard by grew the true lover's primrofe, whofe kind favour wifheth men to be faithful and women courteous. Alongft in a border grew maidenhair, fit for modeft maidens to behold and immodeft to blufh at, becaufe it praifeth the one for their natural treffes and condemneth the other for their beaftly and counterfeit periwigs. There was the gentle gilliflower, that wives fhould wear if they were not too froward ; and loyal lavender : but that was full of cuckoo-fpits, to fhew that women's light thoughts make their hufband's heavy heads. There were fweet lilies, God's plenty, which fhewed fair virgins need not weep for wooers, and ftore of balm which could cure ftrange wounds, only not that wound which women receive. . . . ('A Quip for an Upftart Courtier' [1592], xi., pp. 218, 219.) [On the daify *cf.* Ophelia in 'Hamlet,' IV., vi.—G.]

THE ENGLISH FOP AND FLORENTINE CONTEMPOR-ARIES.

In truth, quoth Farneze, I have feen an Englifh gentleman fo diffufed in his fuits, his doublet being for the wear of Caftile, his hofe for Venice, his hat for France, his cloak for Germany, that he feemed no way to be an Englifhman but by the face. And, quoth Peratio, to this are we Florentines almoft grown : for we muft have our courtefies fo cringed, our conges delivered with fuch a long accent, our fpeeches fo affected, as comparing our conditions with the lives of our anceftors, we feem fo far to differ from their former eftate, that did Ovid live, he would make a fecond Metamor-phofis of our eftate. ('Farewell to Folly' [1591], ix., p. 253.)

Country Lad Full Dreſſed.

She met with a wealthy farmer's ſon, who, handſomely decked up in his holiday hoſe, was going very mannerly to be foreman in a Morice dance, and as near as I can gueſs was thus apparelled. He was a tall, ſlender youth, clean made, with a good, indifferent face, having on his head a ſtraw hat ſteeple-wiſe, bound about with a band of blue buckram. He had on his father's beſt tawny jacket : for that this day's exploit ſtood upon his credit. He was in a pair of hoſe of red kerſey, cloſe truſſed with a point afore ; his mother had lent him a new muffler for a napkin, and that was tied to his girdle for looſing. He had a pair of harveſt gloves on his hands, as ſhewing good huſbandry, and a pen and ink-horn at his back ; for the young man was a little bookiſh. His pumps [= ſhoes] were a little too heavy, being trimmed ſtart-ups made of a pair of boot legs tied before with two white leather thongs. Thus handſomely arrayed, for this was his Sunday ſuit, he met the lady Mæſia, and ſeeing her ſo fair and well-formed, far paſſing their country maids in proportion, and nothing differing in apparel, he ftood half amazed, as a man that had feen a creature beyond his country conceit. ('Farewell to Folly' [1591], ix., pp. 265, 266.)

IDLENESS.

The man coveting, although he were poor, to be counted virtuous, firft efchewed idlenefs, the moth that foreft and fooneft infecteth the mind with many mifchiefs, and applied himfelf fo to his works, being a fmith, that he thought no victuals to have that tafte which were not purchafed by his own fweat. ('Perimedes' [1588], vii., pp. 11, 12.)

JEALOUSY.

When gods had framed the fweet of
    women's face,
  And locked men's looks within their
    golden hair,
That Phœbus blufhed to fee their match-
    lefs grace,
  And heavenly gods on earth did make
    repair,

To quip fair Venus' overweening pride,
Love's happy thoughts to Jealoufy were
    tied.

Then grew a wrinkle on fair Venus'
    brow ;
  The amber fweet of love is turned to
    gall ;
Gloomy was heaven ; bright Phœbus
    did avow
  He could be coy, and would not love
    at all ;
Swearing no greater mifchief could be
    wrought
Than love united to a jealous thought.
    ('Ciceronis Amor' [1589], vii., pp.
        123, 124.)

KINGS.

'Uneasy lies the head that wears a crown.'

Bajazet, Emperor of Turkey.

Leave me, my lords, until I call you
    forth,
For I am heavy and difconfolate.
                [*Exit all but Bajazet.*
So, Bajazet, now thou remaineft alone,

Unrip the thoughts that harbour in thy
    breaſt
And eat thee up ; for arbiter here's none
That may defcry the caufe of thy unreſt,
Unleſs thefe walls thy fecret thoughts
    declare :
And princes' walls they fay unfaithful
    are.
Why, that's the profit of great regiment,*
That all of us are fubject unto fears,
And this vain fhew and glorious intent,
Privy fufpicion on each fcruple rears.
Ay, though on all the world we make
    extent,
From the South Pole unto the Northern
    Bears,
And ſtretch our reign from Eaſt to
    Weſtern fhore,
Yet doubt and care are with us ever-
    more.
Look how the earth clad in her fummer's
    pride
Embroidereth her mantle gorgeoufly
With fragrant herbs and flowers gaily
    dyed,
Spreading abroad her fpangled tapeſtry :
Yet under all a loathfome fnake doth
    hide.

            * *government.*

Such is our life; under crowns cares do
  lie,
And fear, the fceptre ftill attends upon.
Oh, who can take delight in kingly
  throne ?
Public diforders joined with private
  cark ;
Care of our friends, and of our children
  dear,
Do tofs our lives, as waves a filly bark.
Though we be fearlefs, 'tis not without
  fear,
For hidden mifchief lurketh in the dark :
And ftorms may fall, be the day ne'er fo
  clear.
He knows not what it is to be a king
That thinks a fceptre is a pleafant thing.
     ('Selimus,' xiv., pp. 195, 196.)

SOLILOQUY OF SELIMUS—USURPER AND TYRANT.

Now, Selimus, confider who thou art ;
Long haft thou march'd in difguif'd
  attire,
But now unmafk thyfelf, and play thy
  part,

And manifeſt the heat of thy deſire ;
Nouriſh the coals of thine ambitious fire;
And think that then thy empire is moſt
    ſure,
When men for fear thy tyranny endure.
Think that to thee there is no worſe
    reproach
Than filial duty in ſo high a place.
Thou ought'ſt to ſet barrels of blood
    abroach,
And ſeek with ſword whole kingdoms to
    diſplace :
Let Mahound's* laws be locked up in
    their caſe,
And meaner men, and of a baſer ſpirit,
In virtuous actions ſeek for glorious
    merit.
I count it ſacrilege for to be holy,
Or reverence this threadbare name of
    good ;
Leave to old men and babes that kind
    of folly,
Count it of equal value with the mud :
Make thou a paſſage for thy guſhing
    flood,
By ſlaughter, treaſon, or what elſe thou
    can,
And ſcorn religion ; it diſgraces man.

    .   .   .   .   .

* *Mahomet.*

Nor pafs I what our holy votaries
Shall here object againft my forward
    mind ;
I reck not of their foolifh ceremonies,
But mean to take my fortune as I find :
Wifdom commands to follow tide and
    wind,
And catch the front of fwift Occafion,
Before fhe be too quickly overgone :
    Some men will fay I am too impious
Thus to lay fiege againft my father's life,
And that I ought to follow virtuous
And godly fons ; that virtue is a glafs
Wherein I may my errant life behold,
And frame myfelf by it in ancient mould.
    Good Sir, your wifdom's overflowing
    wit,
Digs deep with Learning's wonder-
    working fpade :
Perhaps you think that now forfooth
    you fit
With fome grave wizard in a prattling
    fhade.
Avaunt fuch glafses; let them view in me,
The perfect picture of right tyranny.

   .   .   .   .   .

Is he my father ? why, I am his fon ;
I owe no more to him than he to me.

   .   .   .   .   .

But for I fee the Schoolmen are pre-
        par'd
To plant 'gainft me their bookifh ordi-
        nance,
I mean to ftand on a fententious guard;
And without any far-fetched circum-
        ftance,
Quickly unfold mine own opinion,
To arm my heart with Irreligion.
    When firft this circled round, this
        building fair,
Some god took out of the confufèd mafs
(What god I do not know, nor greatly
        care);
Then every man of his own 'dition was,
And everyone his life in peace did
        pafs.
War was not then, and riches were not
        known,
And no man faid this, or this, is mine
        own.
The ploughman with a furrow did not
        mark
How far his great poffeffions did reach;
The earth knew not the fhare, nor feas
        the bark.
The foldiers enter'd not the batter'd
        breach,
Nor trumpets the tantara loud did teach.

There needed then no judge, nor yet
    no law,
Nor any king of whom to ftand in awe.
But after Ninus, warlike Belus' fon,
The earth with unknown armour did
    array,
Then firft the facred name of king begun,
And things that were as common as the
    day,
Did then to fet poffeffors firft obey.
Then they eftablifh'd laws and holy rites,
To maintain peace, and govern bloody
    fights.
Then fome fage man, above the vulgar
    wife,
Knowing that laws could not in quiet
    dwell,
Unlefs they were obferv'd; did firft
    devife
The names of gods, religion, heaven
    and hell,
And 'gan of pains and feign'd rewards
    to tell :
Pains for thofe men which did neglect
    the law,
Rewards for thofe that liv'd in quiet awe.
Whereas indeed they were mere fictions,
And if they were not, Selim thinks they
    were ;

And thefe religious obfervations,
Only bug-bears to keep the world in
     fear,
And make men quietly a yoke to bear.
So that Religion of itfelf a bable,*
Was only found to make us peaceable.
Hence in efpecial come the foolifh names
Of father, mother, brother, and fuch
     like :
For whofo well his cogitation frames,
Shall find they ferve but only for to
     ftrike
Into our minds a certain kind of love.
For thefe names too are but a policy
To keep the quiet of fociety.
     Indeed, I muft confefs they are not
     bad,
Becaufe they keep the bafer fort in fear ;
But we, whofe mind in heavenly thoughts
     is clad ;
Whofe body doth a glorious fpirit bear ;
That hath no bounds, but flieth every-
     where ;
Why fhould we feek to make that foul a
     flave,
To which dame Nature fo large freedom
     gave ?
Amongft us men there is fome difference

         * *bauble.*

Of actions, termèd by us good or ill :
As he that doth his father recompence,
Differs from him that doth his father
  kill.
And yet I think, think other what they
  will,
That parricides, when death hath given
  them reſt,
Shall have as good a part as have the
  beſt ;
And that's juſt nothing : for as I ſuppoſe
In death's void kingdom reigns eternal
  night :
Secure of evil, and ſecure of foes,
Where nothing doth the wicked man
  affright,
No more than him that dies in doing
  right.
Then ſince in death nothing ſhall to us
  fall,
Here while I live, I'll have a ſnatch at
  all ;
And that can never, never be attain'd
Unleſs old Bajazet do die the death.
        ('Selimus,' xiv., pp. 201-206.)

Selimus again alone—defeated.

Shall Selim's hope be buried in the duft?
And Bajazet triumph over his fall?
Then oh, thou blindful miftrefs of
　mifhap,
Chief patronefs of Rhamus'* golden gates,
I will advance my ftrong revenging hand,
And pluck thee from thy ever-turning
　wheel.
Mars, or Minerva, Mahound, Terma-
　gunt,
Or whofoe'er you are that fight 'gainft me,
Come, and but fhow yourfelves before
　my face,
And I will rend you all like trembling
　reeds.
　　Well, Bajazet, though Fortune fmile
　　on thee,
And deck thy camp with glorious
　victory;
Though Selimus now conquered by thee
Is fain to put his fafety in fwift flight;
Yet fo he flies, that like an angry ram
He'll turn more fiercely than before he
　came.
　　　　　　　　(*Ibid.*, p. 218.)

* Misprinted so for Rhamnus＝Ramnusia,
surname of Nemesis.—G.

JONAH'S APPEAL TO LONDON AND ENGLAND.

You Iflanders, on whom the milder air
Doth fweetly breathe the balm of kind
    increafe ;
Whofe lands are fatt'ned with the dew
    of Heaven,
And made more fruitful than Aĕtean
    plains ;
You, whom delicious pleafures dandle
    foft ;
Whofe eyes are blinded with fecurity ;
Unmafk yourfelves, caft error clean
    afide.
    O, London, maiden of the miftrefs
    Ifle,
Wrapt in the folds and fwathing clouts
    of fhame,
In thee more fins than Nineveh con-
    tains :
Contempt of God, defpite of reverend
    age,
Neglect of law, defire to wrong the
    poor,
Corruption, whoredom, drunkennefs,
    and pride.
Swollen are thy brows with impudence
    and fhame :

O, proud, adulterous glory of the Weft,
Thy neighbours burn, yet doft thou fear
    no fire ;
Thy preachers cry, yet doft thou ftop
    thine ears ;
The 'larum rings, yet fleepeth thou
    fecure.
London, awake, for fear the Lord do
    frown.
I fet a looking-glafs before thine eyes,
O turn, O turn, with weeping to the
    Lord,
And think the prayers and virtues of
    thy Queen*
Defers the plague which otherwife
    would fall.
Repent, O London, left for thine offence,
Thy fhepherd fail, whom mighty God
    preferve :
That fhe may 'bide the pillar of the
    Church
Againft the ftorms of Romifh anti-Chrift;
The hand of mercy overfhed her head ;
And let all faithful fubjects say Amen.
('A Looking-glafs for London and Eng-
    land' [1594], xiv., pp. 112, 113.)

    * Elizabeth.—G.

DISPRAISE OF LOVE.

Some fay Love,
 Foolifh Love,
Doth rule and govern all the gods :
I fay Love,
 Inconftant Love,
Sets men's fenfes far at odds.
Some fwear Love,
 Smooth-fac'd Love,
Is fweeteft fweet that men can have :
I fay Love,
 Sour Love,
Makes Virtue yield as Beauty's flave :
A bitter fweet, a folly worft of all,
That forceth Wifdom to be Folly's thrall.

Love fweet :
 Wherein fweet ?
In fading pleafures that do pain.
Beauty fweet :
 Is that fweet,
That yieldeth forrow for a gain ?
If Love's fweet,
 Herein fweet,
That minutes' joys are monthly woes :
'Tis not fweet,
 That is fweet
Nowhere but where repentance grows :

Then love who lift, if Beauty be fo four ;
Labour for me, Love reft in prince's
     bower.
(' Menaphon ' [1589], vi., pp. 41, 42.)

LOVE (= *Cupid as child*).

Fond, feigning poets make of love a god,
  And leave the laurel for the myrtle-
    boughs
When Cupid is a child not paft the rod,
  And fair Diana Daphne moft allows :
I'll wear the bays, and call the wag a
    boy,
And think of love but as a foolifh toy.

Some give him bow and quiver at his
    back ;
  Some make him blind to aim without
    advice ;
When, naked wretch, fuch feathered
    bolts he lack
  And fight he hath, but cannot wrong
    the wife ;
For ufe but labour's weapon for defence,
And Cupid, like a coward, flieth thence.

He's god in Court, but cottage calls him
    child ;
    And Vefta's virgins with their holy
    fires
Do cleanfe the thoughts that fancy hath
    defiled,
    And burn the palace of his fond
    defires ;
With chafte difdain they fcorn the foolifh
    god,
And prove him but a boy not paft the
    rod.
('Ciceronis Amor' [1589], vii., p. 136.)

LOVE'S TREACHERY.*

Cupid abroad was 'lated in the night,
    His wings were wet with ranging in
    the rain ;
Harbour he fought, to me he took his
    flight,
    To dry his plumes : I heard the boy
    complain ;
I oped the door, and granted his defire ;
I rofe myfelf, and made the wag a fire.

    * After Anacreon. Another slightly variant
text in 'Alcida' (1588).

Looking more narrow by the fire's flame,
  I fpied his quiver hanging by his
    back :
Doubting the boy might my misfortune
    frame,
  I would have gone for fear of further
    wrack ;
But what I drad, did me, poor wretch,
    betide ;
For forth he drew an arrow from his
    fide.

He pierced the quick, and I began to
    ftart ;
  A pleafing wound, but that it was too
    high ;
His fhaft procured a fharp yet fugared
    fmart :
  Away he flew, for why* his wings
    were dry ;
But left the arrow fticking in my breaft,
That fore I grieved I welcomed fuch a
    gueft.
    ('The Orpharion' [1589], xii., pp.
      73, 74.)

* *because.*

DORON'S DESCRIPTION OF SAMELA.

Like to Diana in her fummer-weed,
Girt with a crimfon robe of brighteft
    dye,
             Goes fair Samela ;
Whiter than be the flocks that ftraggling
    feed,
When wafhed by Arethufa, faint* they
    lie,
             Is fair Samela ;
As fair Aurora in her morning grey,
Decked with the ruddy glifter of her
    love,
             Is fair Samela ;
Like lovely Thetis on a calmèd day,
Whenas her brightnefs Neptune's fancy
    move,
             Shines fair Samela ;
Her treffes gold, her eyes like glaffy
    ftreams ;
Her teeth are pearl, the breafts are ivory ;
             Of fair Samela ;

* Sidney Walker plausibly proposes 'fount ;'
but 'faint' is the undoubted reading, and
yields an excellent sense.—G.

Her cheeks, like rose and lily, yield
    forth gleams ;
Her brows bright arches framed of ebony:
       Thus fair Samela
'Passeth fair Venus in her bravest hue,
And Juno in the show of majesty :
       For she's Samela ;
Pallas in wit, all three if you will view,
For beauty, wit, and matchless dignity,
       Yield to Samela.
('Menaphon' [1589], vi., pp. 65, 66.)

N'OSEREZ VOUS, MON BEL AMI?

Sweet Adon, darest not glance thine
    eye,—
    N'oserez vous, mon bel ami ?—
Upon thy Venus that must die ?
    Je vous en prie, pity me ;
N'oserez vous, mon bel, mon bel,
N'oserez vous, mon bel ami ?

See how sad thy Venus lies,—
    N'oserez vous, mon bel ami ?—
Love in heart, and tears in eyes ;
    Je vous en prie, pity me ;

N'oferez vous, mon bel, mon bel,
N'oferez vous, mon bel ami ?

Thy face as fair as Paphos' brooks,—
   N'oferez vous, mon bel ami ?—
Wherein Fancy baits her hooks ;
   Je vous en prie, pity me ;
N'oferez vous, mon bel, mon bel,
N'oferez vous, mon bel ami ?

Thy cheeks, like cherries that do grow,—
   N'oferez vous, mon bel ami ?—
Amongft the Weftern mounts of fnow ;
   Je vous en prie, pity me ;
N'oferez vous, mon bel, mon bel,
N'oferez vous, mon bel ami ?

Thy lips vermilion, full of love,—
   N'oferez vous, mon bel ami ?—
Thy neck as filver-white as dove ;
   Je vous en prie, pity me ;
N'oferez vous, mon bel, mon bel,
N'oferez vous, mon bel ami ?

Thine eyes, like flames of holy fires,—
   N'oferez vous, mon bel ami ?—
Burn all my thoughts with fweet defires ;
   Je vous en prie, pity me ;
N'oferez vous, mon bel, mon bel,
N'oferez vous, mon bel ami ?—

All thy beauties sting my heart ;—
   N'oserez vous, mon bel ami ?—
I must die through Cupid's dart ;
   Je vous en prie, pity me ;
N'oserez vous, mon bel, mon bel,
N'oserez vous, mon bel ami ?

Wilt thou let thy Venus die ?—
   N'oserez vous, mon bel ami ?—
Adon were unkind, say I,—
   Je vous en prie, pity me ;
N'oserez vous, mon bel, mon bel,
N'oserez vous, mon bel ami ?

To let fair Venus die for woe,—
   N'oserez vous, mon bel ami ?—
That doth love sweet Adon so ;
   Je vous en prie, pity me ;
N'oserez vous, mon bel, mon bel,
N'oserez vous, mon bel ami ?
   ('Never Too Late' [1590], viii., pp.
     75, 76.)

EURYMACHUS' FANCY IN THE PRIME OF HIS AFFECTION.

When lordly Saturn, in a fable robe,
Sat full of frowns and mourning in the
    Weft ;
The evening ftar fcarce peeped from
    out her lodge,
And Phœbus newly galloped to his reft ;
        Even then
        Did I
Within my boat fit in the filent ftreams,
All void of cares as he that lies and
    dreams.

As Phao, fo a ferryman I was ;
The country-laffes faid I was too fair :
With eafy toil I laboured at mine oar,
To pafs from fide to fide who did repair ;
        And then
        Did I
For pains take pence, and, Charon-like,
    tranfport
As foon the fwain as men of high
    import.

When want of work did give me leave
    to reft,
My fport was catching of the wanton
    fifh :

So did I wear the tedious time away,
And with my labour mended oft my
    difh ;
        For why*
        I thought
That idle hours were calendars of
    ruth,
And time ill-fpent was prejudice to
    youth.

I fcorned to love ; for were the nymph
    as fair
As fhe that loved the beauteous Latmian
    fwain ;
Her face, her eyes, her treffes, nor her
    brows
Like ivory could my affection gain ;
        For why
        I faid
With high difdain, 'Love is a bafe
    defire,
And Cupid's flames, why, they're but
    watery fire.'

As thus I fat, difdaining of proud love,
'Have over, ferryman !' there cried a
    boy ;

        * *because.*

And with him was a paragon for
    hue,
A lovely damfel, beauteous and coy ;
       And there
       With her
A maiden, covered with a tawny veil ;
Her face unfeen for breeding lover's
    bale.

I fteered my boat, and when I came to
    fhore,
The boy was winged ; methought it
    was a wonder ;
The dame had eyes like lightning, or
    the flafh
That runs before the hot report of
    thunder ;
       Her fmiles
       Were fweet,
Lovely her face ; was ne'er fo fair a
    creature ;
For earthly carcafe had a heavenly
    feature.

' My friend,' quoth fhe, ' fweet ferry-
    man, behold,
We three muft pafs, but not a farthing
    fare ;

But I will give, for I am Queen of
　　love,
The brighteſt laſs thou lik'ſt unto thy
　　ſhare ;
　　　　Chooſe where
　　　　Thou loveſt,
Be ſhe as fair as Love's ſweet lady is,
She ſhall be thine, if that will be thy
　　bliſs.'

With that ſhe ſmiled with ſuch a pleaſing
　　face
As might have made the marble rock
　　relent ;
But I, that triumphed in diſdain of
　　love,
Bade fie on him that to fond love was
　　bent :
　　　　And then
　　　　Said thus,
' So light the ferryman for love doth
　　care,
As Venus paſs not if ſhe pay no fare.'

At this a frown ſat on her angry
　　brow ;
She winks upon her wanton ſon hard
　　by ;
He from his quiver drew a bolt of fire,

And aimed fo right as that he pierced
   mine eye ;
      And then
      Did fhe
Draw down the veil that hid the virgin's
   face,
Whofe heavenly beauty lightened all the
   place.*

Straight then I leaned mine arm upon
   mine oar,
And looked upon the nymph (if fo†) was
   fair ;
Her eyes were ftars, and like Apollo's
   locks
Methought appeared the trammels of
   her hair :
      Thus did
      I gaze,
And fucked in beauty, till that fweet
   defire
Caft fuel on, and fet my thoughts on fire.

When I was lodged within the net of
   love,
And thus they faw my heart was all on
   flame ;

  * Spenser probably inspired this exquisite
fancy.—G.
  † Query, *if she ?*

The nymph away, and with her trips
    along
The wingèd boy, and with her goes his
    dame :
        O, then
        I cried,
' Stay, ladies, ſtay, and take not any care,
You all ſhall paſs, and pay no penny
    fare.'

Away they fling, and looking coyly back,
They laugh at me, O, with a loud diſ-
    dain !
I ſend out ſighs to overtake the nymphs,
And tears, as lures, to call them back
    again ;
        But they
        Fly thence ;
But I ſit in my boat, with hand on oar,
And feel a pain, but know not what's
    the ſore.

At laſt I feel it is the flame of love ;
I ſtrive, but bootleſs, to expreſs the pain;
It cools, it fires, it hopes, it fears, it frets,
And ſtirreth paſſions throughout every
    vein ;
        That down
        I ſat,

And fighing did fair Venus' laws approve,
And fwore no thing fo fweet and four
as love.
(' Francefco's Fortunes ; or, the Second
Part of Never too Late ' [1590], viii.,
pp. 175-179.)

LOVE.

Mullidor's Madrigal.

Dildido, dildido,
O love, O love,
I feel thy rage rumble below and above!

In fummer-time I faw a face,
Trop belle pour moi, hélas, hélas!
Like to a ftoned-horfe was her pace :
Was ever young man fo difmayed ?
Her eyes, like wax-torches, did make
me afraid :
Trop belle pour moi, voilà mon trépas.

Thy beauty, my love, exceedeth fup-
pofes ;
Thy hair is a nettle for the niceft rofes.
Mon dieu, aide moi!

That I with the primrose of my fresh
  wit
May tumble her tyranny under my feet:
Hé donc je serai un jeune roi !
Trop belle pour moi, hélas, hélas !
Trop belle pour moi, voilà mon trépas.
('Francesco's Fortunes; or, the Second
  part of Never too Late,' viii., p. 217.)

PASSIONATE LOVERS.

Whoso readeth the Romish Records
and Grecian Histories, and turneth over
the volumes filled with the reports of
passionate lovers, shall find sundry son-
nets sauced with sorrowful passions,
divers ditties declaring their dumps,
careful complaints, woeful wailings, and
a thousand sundry hapless motions,
wherein the poor perplexed lovers do
point out how the beauty of their mistress
hath amazed their minds, how their
fancy is fettered with their exquisite
perfection, how they are snared with the
form of her feature [= person], how the
gifts of Nature so bountifully bestowed
upon her hath entangled their minds

and bewitched their senses : that her
excellent virtue, and singular bounty
hath so charmed their affections, and
her rare qualities hath so drowned them
in desire, as they esteem her courtesy
more than Cæsar's kingdoms, her love
more than lordships, and her good will
more than all worldly wealth.   Tush,
all treasure is but trash in respect of her
person.   ('Morando' [1587], iii., pp.
63, 64.)

EURYMACHUS IN PRAISE OF MIRIMIDA.

When Flora, proud in pomp of all her
    flowers,
       Sat bright and gay,
And gloried in the dew of Iris showers,
       And did display
Her mantle chequered all with gaudy
    green :
       Then I
       Alone
A mournful man in Erecine was seen.

With folded arms I trampled through
     the graſs,
         Tracing, as he
That held the Throne of Fortune brittle
     glaſs,
         And love to be
Like fortune fleeting, as the reſtleſs wind
         Mixed
         With miſts,
Whoſe damp doth make the cleareſt eyes
     grow blind.

Thus in a maze I ſpied a hideous flame :
         I caſt my ſight,
And ſaw where blythely bathing in the
     ſame,
         With great delight,
A worm did lie, wrapt in a ſmoky ſweat :
         And yet
         'Twas ſtrange
It careleſs lay, and ſhrunk not at the
     heat.

I ſtood amazed, and wondering at the
     ſight,
         While that a dame
That ſhone like to the heaven's rich
     ſparkling light,
         Diſcourſed the ſame :

And ſaid, My friend, this worm within
    the fire
        Which lies
        Content,
Is Venus' worm, and reprefents Deſire.

A Salamander is this princely beaſt,
        Deck'd with a crown,
Given him by Cupid, as a gorgeous
    creſt
        'Gainſt Fortune's frown :
Content he lies, and bathes him in the
    flame,
        And goes
        Not forth :
For why he cannot live without the
    ſame.

As he : ſo lovers lie within the fire
        Of fervent love,
And ſhrink not from the flame of hot
    deſire,
        Nor will not move
From any heat that Venus' force im-
    parts :
        But lie
        Content
Within a fire, and waſte away their
    hearts.

Up flew the dame, and vanifh'd in a
    cloud,
        But there ftood I,
And many thoughts within my mind did
    fhroud
        Of love : for why
I felt within my heart a fcorching fire,
        And yet
        As did
The Salamander, 'twas my whole defire.
    ('Never too Late' [1590], viii., pp.
        207-209.)

LOVE—WHAT?

What thing is love ?   It is a power divine
That reigns in us ; or elfe a wreakful
    law
That dooms our minds to beauty to in-
    cline :
It is a ftar, whofe influence doth draw
    Our hearts to Love, diffembling of
    his might,
        Till he be mafter of our hearts and
        fight.

Love is a difcord, and a ftrange divorce
Betwixt our fenfe and reafon, by whofe
    power,
As mad with reafon, we admit that force,
Which wit or labour never may devour.
    It is a will that brooketh no confent :
    It would refufe, yet never may repent.

Love's a defire, which for to wait a time,
Doth lofe an age of years, and fo doth
    pafs,
As doth the fhadow fever'd from his
    prime,
Seeming as though it were, yet never
    was :
    Leaving behind nought but repentant
    thoughts
    Of days ill fpent, for that which
    profits noughts.

It's now a peace, and then a fudden war ;
A hope confum'd before it is conceiv'd ;
At hand it fears, and menaceth afar,
And he that gains is moft of all deceiv'd :
    It is a fecret hidden and not known,
    Which one may better feel than write
    upon.
('Menaphon' [1589], vi., pp. 140, 141.)

GENTLE COURTSHIPS REJECTED.

Grime. I fay, Sir Gilbert, looking on my daughter,
I curfe the hour that ever I got the girl :
For, Sir, fhe may have many wealthy fuitors,
And yet fhe difdains them all,
To have poor George a Greene unto her hufband.

    Bonfield. On that, good Grime, I am talking with thy daughter ;
But fhe, in quirks and quiddities of love,
Sets me to fchool, fhe is fo over-wife.
But, gentle girl, if thou wilt forfake the Pinner,
And be my love, I will advance thee high :
To dignify thofe hairs of amber hue,
I'll grace them with a chaplet made of pearl,
Set with choice rubies, fparks, and diamonds
Planted upon a velvet hood, to hide that head
Wherein two fapphires burn like fparkling fire :

This will I do, fair Bettris, and far more,
If thou wilt love the Lord of Doncaſter.
   Bettris. Heigh ho, my heart is in a
    higher place,
Perhaps on the earl, if that be he :
See where he comes, or angry, or in
   love ;
For why, his colour looketh diſcontent.
('George a Greene, the Pinner of Wake-
   field' [1599], xiv., pp. 131, 132.)

GEORGE A GREENE AND BEATRICE (BETTRIS).

   George. Tell me, ſweet love, how is
    thy mind content ?
What, canſt thou brook to live with
   George a Greene ?
   Bettris. Oh, George, how little pleaſ-
    ing are theſe words ?
Came I from Bradford for the love of
   thee,
And left my father for ſo ſweet a friend?
Here will I live until my life do end.
   George. Happy am I to have ſo ſweet
    a love.
              (*Ibid.,* p. 168.)

LOVE-SUPPLANTER.

Edward, Prince of Wales.
Lacy, Earl of Lincoln.

Enter Prince Edward, with his poniard in his hand: Lacy and Margaret.

Edward. Lacy, thou canſt not ſhroud thy traitrous thoughts,
Nor cover, as did Caſſius, all his wiles ;
For Edward hath an eye that looks as far
As Linceus from the ſhores of Grecia.
Did not I ſit in Oxford by the friar,
And ſee thee court the maid of Freſing-field,
Sealing thy flattering fancies with a kiſs ?
Did not proud Bungay draw his portaſſe
  ｉ forth,
And joining hand in hand had married you,
If Friar Bacon had not ſtrook him dumb,
And mounted him upon a ſpirit's back,
That we might chat at Oxford with the friar ?
Traitor, what anſwereſt, is not all this true ?
  Lacy. Truth all, my lord, and thus I make reply :

At Harlſtone Fair there courting for
    your grace,
Whenas mine eye ſurvey'd her curious
    ſhape,*
And drew the beauteous glory of her
    looks,
To dive into the centre of my heart ;
Love taught me that your honour did
    but jeſt,
That princes were in fancy but as men :
How that the lovely maid of Freſingfield
Was fitter to be Lacy's wedded wife,
Than concubine unto the Prince of
    Wales.
    Edward. Injurious Lacy, did I love
    thee more
Than Alexander his Hepheſtion ?
Did I unfold the paſſion of my love,
And lock them in the cloſet of thy
    thoughts ?
Wert thou to Edward ſecond to himſelf,
Sole friend, and partner of his ſecret
    loves ?
And could a glance of fading beauty
    break
Th'inchainèd fetters of ſuch private
    friends ?

    * *curiosity-exciting ſhape.*

Bafe coward, false, and too effeminate,
To be co-rival with a prince in thoughts:
From Oxford have I pofted fince I dined,
To 'quite a traitor 'fore that Edward fleep.
    Margaret. 'Twas I, my lord, not
         Lacy ftepp'd awry,
For oft he fued and courted for yourfelf,
And ftill woo'd for the courtier all in
       green ;
But I whom fancy made but overfond,
Pleaded myfelf with looks as if I lov'd ;
I fed mine eye with gazing on his face,
And ftill bewitch'd, lov'd Lacy with my
       looks :
My heart with fighs, mine eyes pleaded
       with tears,
My face held pity and content at once,
And more I could not cipher out by
       figns,
But that I lov'd Lord Lacy with my
       heart.
Then, worthy Edward, meafure with
       thy mind,
If women's favours will not force men
       fall ;
If beauty, and if darts of piercing love
Is not of force to bury thoughts of
       friends. . . .
         ('Friar Bacon,' xiii., pp. 49-51.)

LOVE NO MORTAL PASSION.

Truly, fir (quoth Panthia), to fpeak my mind freely without affeſtation, in this cafe this is my opinion. That love being no mortal paſſion, but a fuper-natural influence allotted unto every man by Deſtiny, charmeth and en-chanteth the minds of mortal creatures, not according to their wills, but as the decree of the Fates ſhall determine, for fome are in love at the firſt look. As was Perfeus with Andromeda. Some never to be reclaimed, as was Narciſſus. Others fcorched at the firſt fight, as Venus herfelf was of Adonis. Some always proclaim open wars to Cupid, as did Daphne. Thus I conclude, that men or women are no more or lefs fub-jeſt unto love, refpeſting their natural conſtitution, but by the fecret influence of a certain fupernatural conſtellation. ('Morando' [1587], iii., p. 108.)

SILVESTRO'S LADY-LOVE.

Her ſtature like the tall ſtraight cedar-
trees,
Whoſe ſtately bulks doth fame th' Arabian
groves ;
A face like princely Juno when ſhe
braved
The Queen of Love 'fore Paris in the
vale :
A front beſet with love and courteſy ;
A face like modeſt Pallas when ſhe
bluſh'd
A ſilly ſhepherd ſhould be Beauty's
judge :
A lip ſweet ruby red, grac'd with delight;
A cheek wherein for interchange of hue
A wrangling ſtrife 'twixt lily and the
roſe :
Her eyes, two twinkling ſtars in Winter
nights,
When chilling froſt doth clear the azur'd
ſky ;
Her hair of golden hue doth dim the
beams
That proud Apollo giveth from his
coach :
The Gnydian doves, whoſe white and
ſnowy pens

Doth ftain the filver-ftreaming ivory,
May not compare with thofe two moving
   hills
Which, topt with pretty teats, difcovers
   down a vale
Wherein the god of love may deign to
   fleep ;
A foot like Thetis when fhe tript the
   lands
To fteal Neptune's favour with her fteps.
   (' Tritameron,' 2nd pt. [1587], iii.,
                              p. 123.)

MENALCAS—THE PRODIGAL'S RETURN.

The filent fhade had fhadowed every
   tree,
And Phœbus in the weft was fhrouded
   low ;
Each hive had home her bufy labouring
   bee ;
Each bird the harbour of the night did
   know :
         Even then,
         When thus

All things did from their weary labour
    lin,
Menalcas fate and thought him of his
    fin.

His head on hand, his elbow on his
    knee,
And tears, like dew, bedrench'd upon
    his face ;
His face as fad as any fwain's might be ;
His thoughts and dumps befitting well
    the place :
        Even then,
        When thus
Menalcas fate in paffions all alone,
He sighèd then, and thus he 'gan to
    moan.

I that fed flocks upon Theffalia's plains
And bade my lambs to feed on daffodil,
That liv'd on milk and curds, poor
    fhepherd's gains,
And merry fate, and pip'd upon a
    pleafant hill.
        Even then,
        When thus
I fate fecure and fear'd not Fortune's
    ire,
Mine eyes eclipf'd, faft blinded by defire.

Then lofty thoughts began to lift my
    mind ;
I grudg'd and thought my fortune was
    too low ;
A fhepherd's life 'twas bafe and out of
    kind ;
The talleſt cedars have the faireſt grow.
        Even then,
        When thus
Pride did intend the fequel of my ruth,
Began the faults and follies of my
    youth.

I left the fields, and took me to the
    town ;
Fold fheep who liſt, the hook was caſt
    away,
Menalcas would not be a country clown,
Nor fhepherd's weeds, but garments far
    more gay :
        Even then,
        When thus
Afpiring thoughts did follow after ruth,
Began the faults and follies of my youth.

My fuits were filk, my talk was all of
    State ;
I ſtretch'd beyond the compaſs of my
    fleeve ;

The braveſt courtier was Menalcas'
    mate ;
Spend what I would, I never thought
    on grief.
            Even then,
            When thus
I laſh'd out laviſh, then began my ruth,
And then I felt the follies of my
    youth.

I caſt mine eye on every wanton face,
And ſtraight deſire did hale me on to
    love ;
Then, lover-like, I pray'd for Venus'
    grace,
That ſhe my miſtreſs' deep affects might
    move :
            Even then,
            When thus
Love trapp'd me in the fatal bands of
    ruth,
Began the faults and follies of my youth.

No coſt I ſpar'd to pleaſe my miſtreſs'
    eye ;
No time ill ſpent in preſence of her
    ſight ;
Yet oft ſhe frown'd, and then her love
    muſt die,

But when fhe smil'd, oh then a happy
    wight :
        Even then,
        When thus
Defire did draw me on to deem of ruth,
Began the faults and follies of my youth.

The day in poems often did I pafs,
The night in fighs and forrows for her
    grace ;
And fhe as fickle as the brittle glafs,
Held funfhine fhowers within her flatter-
    ing face :
        Even then,
        When thus
I fpied the woes that women's love
    enfueth,
I faw, and loath'd the follies of my youth.

I noted oft that beauty was a blaze ;
I faw that love was but a heap of cares ;
That fuch as ftood as deer do at the gaze,
And fought their wealth amongft affec-
    tion's fnares ;
        Even fuch,
        I faw,
With hot purfuit did follow after ruth,
And foftered up the follies of their
    youth.

Thus clogg'd with love, with paffions
    and with grief,
I faw the country life had leaft moleft ;
I felt a wound and pain would have
    relief,
And thus refolv'd, I thought would fall
    out beft :
          Even then,
          When thus
I felt my fenfes almoft fold to ruth,
I thought to leave the follies of my youth.

To flocks again, away the wanton town ;
Fond pride, avaunt, give me the fhep-
    herd's hook ;
A coat of gray, I'll be a country clown :
Mine eye fhall fcorn on beauty for to
    look :
          No more,
          A-do :
Both pride and love, are ever pain'd*
    with ruth,
And therefore farewell the follies of my
    youth.
    (' Mourning Garment ' [1590], ix.,
                pp. 214-218.)

        * *pair'd* (?)

*M*ISERRIMUS.

Deceiving world, that with alluring toys
- Haſt made my life the ſubjeȼt of thy
  ſcorn,
And ſcorneſt now to lend thy fading
  joys
    T'outlength my life, whom friends
    have left forlorn ;
    How well are they that die ere they
    be born,
And never ſee thy ſleights, which few
  men ſhun
Till unawares they helpleſs are un-
  done !

Oft have I ſung of Love and of his
  fire ;
    But now I find that poet was adviſed
Which made full feaſts increaſers of
  deſire,
    And proves weak love was with the
    poor deſpiſed ;
    For when the life with food is not
    ſufficed,
What thoughts of Love, what motion
  of delight,
What pleaſance can proceed from ſuch
  a wight ?

Witnefs my want, the murderer of my
  wit,
    My ravifhed fenfe, of wonted fury
      reft,
Wants fuch conceit, as fhould in poems
  fit,
    Set down the forrow wherein I am
      left :
    But therefore have high heavens their
      gifts bereft,
Becaufe fo long they lent them me to
  ufe,
And I fo long their bounty did abufe.

O, that a year were granted me to live,
    And for that year my former wit
      reftored !
What rules of life, what counfel would
    I give,
    How fhould my fin with forrow be
      deplored !
    But I muft die of every man abhorred :
Time loofely fpent will not again be
  won ;
My time is loofely fpent, and I un-
  done.
(' Groat's-worth of Wit, bought with a
  Million of Repentance ' [1592], xii.,
  pp. 137, 138.)

PALMER'S ODE.

Down the valley 'gan he track,
Bag and bottle at his back,
In a furcoat all of gray ;
Such wear Palmers on the way,
When with fcrip and ftaff they fee
Jefus' grave on Calvary.
A hat of ftraw like a fwain
Shelter for the fun and rain,
With a fcollop fhell before :
Sandals on his feet he wore ;
Legs were bare, arms unclad ;
Such attire this Palmer had.
His face fair like Titan's fhine,
Gray and buxom were his eyne,
Whereout dropt pearls of forrow :
Such fweet tears Love doth borrow,
When in outward dews fhe plains
Heart's diftrefs that lovers pains :
Ruby lips, cherry cheeks :
Such rare mixture Venus feeks,
When to keep her damfels quiet
Beauty fets them down their diet :
Adon was not thought more fair.
Curled locks of amber hair—
Locks where Love did fit and twine
Nets to fnare the gazer's eyne :

Such a Palmer ne'er was feen,
Lefs love himfelf had Palmer been,
Yet for all he was fo quaint
Sorrow did his vifage taint.*
Midft the riches of his face,
Grief decipher'd his difgrace,
Every ftep ftrain'd a tear,
Sudden fighs fhow'd his fear :
And yet his fear by his fight,
Ended in a ftrange delight.
That his paffions did approve,
Weeds and forrow were for love.
(Greene's 'Never too Late' [1590], viii.,
pp. 13-15.)

ANOTHER OF THE SAME.

Old Menalcas on a day,
As in field this fhepherd lay,
Tuning of his oaten pipe,
Which he hit with many a ftripe ;
Said to Corydon that he
Once was young and full of glee :
Blythe and wanton was I then,
Such defires follow men.

* *tint.*

As I lay and kept my fheep,
Came the god that hateth fleep,
Clad in armour all of fire,
Hand in hand with Queen Defire :
And with a dart that wounded nigh,
Pierc'd my heart as I did'lie :
That when I woke I 'gan fwear,
Phillis' beauty palm did bear.
Up I ftart, forth went I
With her face to feed mine eye :
There I faw Defire fit,
That my heart with love had hit,
Laying forth bright Beauty's hooks
To entrap my gazing looks.
Love I did, and 'gan to woo,
Pray and figh ; all would not do :
Women when they take the toy*
Covet to be counted coy.
Coy fhe was, and I 'gan court ;
She thought love was but a fport.
Profound Hell was in my thought :
Such a pain Defire had wrought,
That I fued with fighs and tears.
Still ingrate fhe ftopt her ears
Till my youth I had fpent.
Laft a paffion of repent,
Told me flat that Defire,

* *trifling, playing.*

Was a brand of Love's fire,
Which confumeth men in thrall,
Virtue, youth, wit, and all.
At this faw back I ſtart,
But Defire from my heart,
Shook off Love ; and made an oath,
To be enemy to both.
Old I was when thus I fled,
Such fond toys as cloy'd my head.
But this I learn'd at Virtue's gate,
The way to good is never late.

(Ibid., pp. 17-19.)

THE PENITENT PALMER'S ODE.

Whilom in the Winter's rage
A Palmer old and full of age,
Sat and thought upon his youth,
With eyes, tears, and heart of ruth :
Being all with cares yblent,
When he thought on years miſſpent.
Then his follies came to mind,
How fond love had made him blind,
And wrapt him in a field of woes,
Shadowed with Pleaſure's ſhoes ;
Then he ſighèd and ſaid alas !
Man is fin, and fleſh is graſs.

I thought my miftrefs' hairs were gold,
And in their locks my heart I fold :
Her amber treffes were the fight
That wrappèd me in vain delight :
Her ivory front, her pretty chin,
Were ftales* that drew me on to fin :
Her ftarry looks, her cryftal eyes,
Brighter than the fun's arife :
Sparkling pleafing flames of fire,
Yoked my thoughts and my defire,
That I 'gan cry ere I blin,†
Oh, her eyes are paths to fin !
Her face was fair, her breath was fweet,
All her looks for love was meet :
But love is folly, this I know,
And beauty fadeth like to fnow.
Oh, why fhould man delight in pride,
Whofe bloffom like a dew doth glide ;
When thefe fuppofes touch'd my thought,
That world was vain and beauty nought,
I 'gan figh and fay alas !
Man is fin, and flefh is grafs.

(Ibid., pp. 122, 123.)

* *fnares.*
  † usually explained = *cease :* but qu. = '*grow blind.*'—G.

PASTORAL.

The Defcription of the Shepherd and his Wife.

It was near a thicky fhade
That broad leaves of beech had made ;
Joining all their tops fo nigh
That fcarce Phœbus in could pry,
To fee if lovers in the thick*
Could dally with a wanton trick.
Where fate the fwain and his wife
Sporting in that pleafing life
That Corydon commendeth fo,
All other lives to over-go.
He and fhe did fit and keep
Flocks of kids and folds of fheep :
He upon his pipe did play,
She tun'd voice unto his lay.
And for you might her hufwife know
Voice did fing and fingers few ;
He was young, his coat was green,
With welts† of white, feam'd between,
Turnèd over with a flap
That breaft and bofom in did wrap ;
Skirts fide and pleated‡ free,
Seemly hanging to his knee.

* *thicket.*   † *fringes.*   ‡ *plaited.*

A whittle*ₐwith a filver chape ;†
Cloak was ruffet, and the cape
Servèd for a bonnet oft
To fhroud him from the wet aloft.
A leather fcrip of colour red,
With a button on the head ;
A bottle full of country whig‡
By the fhepherd's fide did lig :§
And in a little bufh hard by
There the fhepherd's dog did lie ;
Who while his mafter 'gan to fleep
Well could watch both kids and fheep.
The fhepherd was a frolic fwain,
For though his 'parell was but plain,
Yet doone‖ the Authors foothly fay
His colour was both frefh and gay ;
And in their writes¶ plain difcufs
Fairer was not Tityrus,
Nor Menalcas, whom they call
The alderleefeft** fwain of all :
'Seeming†† him was his wife,
Both in line‡‡ and in life ;
Fair fhe was as fair might be,
Like the rofes on the tree ;

* *clasp-knife.*   † *clasp.*   ‡ *whey.*
§ *lie.*   ‖ *do.*
¶ *writings,* as, ' *thick* ' for ' *thicket* ' above.
—G.
** *dearest of all.* †† *be-feeming.* ‡‡ *lineage.*

Buxom, blithe, and young, I ween ;
Beauteous, like a Summer's queen :
For her cheeks were ruddy hued
As if lilies were imbrued
With drops of blood, to make the white
Pleafe the eye with more delight ;
Love did lie within her eyes
In ambufh for fome wanton prize :
A leefer* lafs than this had been,
Corydon had never feen ;
Nor was Phillis that fair May
Half fo gaudy or fo gay :†
She wore a chaplet on her head ;
Her caffock was of fcarlet red,
Long and large, as ftraight as bent ;‡
Her middle was both fmall and gent.§
If country loves fuch fweet defires gain,
What lady would not love a fhepherd
     fwain ?
  ('Mourning Garment' [1590], ix.,
    pp. 141-144.)

---

* *dearer.*   † *joyful, bright.*
‡ *grass.*   § *genteel.*

PASTORAL.

The Shephera's Ode.

Walking in a valley green
Spied I Flora, Summer queen :
Where fhe, heaping all her graces,
Niggard feem'd in other places :
Spring it was, and here did fpring
All that Nature forth can bring ;
Groves of pleafant trees there grow,
Which fruit and fhadow could beftow ;
Thick-leaved boughs fmall birds cover
Till fweet notes themfelves difcover ;
Tunes for number feem'd confounded
Whilft their mixture's mufic founded :
Greeing well, yet not agreed
That one the other fhould exceed.
A fweet ftream here filent glides
Whofe clear water no fifh hides ;
Slow it runs, which well bewray'd
The pleafant fhore the current ftay'd :
In this ftream a rock was planted
Where nor art nor nature wanted :
Each thing fo did other grace
As all places may give place ;
Only this the place of pleafure
Where is heapèd Nature's treafure.

Here mine eyes with wonder ftaid,
Eyes amaz'd and mind afraid :
Ravifht with what was beheld,
From departing were withheld.
Mufing then with found advice
On this earthly paradife ;
Sitting by the river fide
Lovely Phillis was defcried :
Gold her hair, bright her eyne
Like to Phœbus in his fhine ;
White her brow, her face was fair,
Amber-breath perfum'd the air ;
Rofe and lily both did feek
To fhew their glory on her cheek.
Love did neftle in her looks,
Baiting there his fharpeft hooks :
Such a Phillis ne'er was feen
More beautiful than Love's queen.
Doubt it was whofe greater grace,
Phillis' beauty, or the place.
Her coat was of fcarlet red,
All in pleats* a mantle fpread :
Fring'd with gold ; a wreath of boughs
To check the fun from her brows.
In her hand a fhepherd's hook,
In her face Diana's look :
Her fheep graz'd on the plains
She had ftolen from the fwains :

* *plaits.*

Under a cool filent fhade,
By the ftreams fhe garlands made.
Thus fate Phillis all alone :
Miffed fhe was by Corydon,
Chiefeft fwain, of all the reft
Lovely Phillis likt him beft.
His face was like Phœbus' love,
His neck white as Venus' dove ;
A ruddy cheek fill'd with fmiles,
Such Love hath when he beguiles :
His locks brown, his eyes were gray,
Like Titan in a Summer day.
A ruffet jacket, fleeves red ;
A blue bonnet on his head ;
A cloak of gray fenc'd the rain ;
Thus 'tyred was this lovely fwain.
A fhepherd's hook her dog tied,
Bag and bottle by his fide :
Such was Paris, fhepherds fay,
When with Œnone he did play.
From his flock ftray'd Corydon,
Spying Phillis all alone :
By the ftream he Phillis fpied,
Braver than was Flora's pride :
Down the valley 'gan he track,
Stole behind his true love's back :
The fun fhone and fhadow made ;
Phillis rofe and was afraid.
When fhe faw her lover there,

Smile fhe did, and left her fear :
Cupid that difdain doth loath
With defire ftrake them both.
The fwain did woo, fhe was nice,
Following fafhion nay'd* him twice :
Much ado he kiff'd her then ;
Maidens blufh when they kifs men :
So did Phillis at that ftowre.†
Her face was like the rofe flower.
Laft they 'greed, for Love would fo,
Faith and troth they would no mo.
For fhepherds ever held it fin
To falfe the love they livèd in.
The fwain gave a girdle red,
She fet garlands on his head.
Gifts were given, they kifs again,
Both did fmile, for both were fain.‡
Thus was love 'mongft fhepherds fold
When fancy knew not what was gold :
They woo'd and vow'd and that they
    keep,
And go contented to their fheep.
    (' Ciceronis Amor' [1589], vii., pp.
               180-184.)

   * *denied.*   † *contention.*   ‡ *fond.*

PHILLIS AND CORIDON.

A Pastoral.

Phillis kept sheep along the Western
    plains,
    And Coridon did feed his flocks hard
        by;
This shepherd was the flower of all the
    swains
    That traced the downs of fruitful
        Thessaly;
And Phillis, that did far her flocks sur-
    pafs
In silver hue, was thought a bonny lafs.

A bonny lafs, quaint in her country 'tire,
    Was lovely Phillis,—Coridon more fo;
Her locks, her looks, did fet the swain
    on fire;
    He left his lambs, and he began to
    woo;
He looked, he fighed, he courted with
    a kifs;
No better could the filly fwad* than this.

He little knew to paint a tale of love;
    Shepherds can fancy, but they cannot
    fay;

        * *swain, clown.*

                                  M 2

Phillis 'gan ſmile, and wily thought to
    prove
  What uncouth* grief poor Coridon
    did pay ;
She aſked him how his flocks or he did
    fare ?
Yet penſive thus his ſighs did tell his
    care.

The ſhepherd bluſhed when Phillis
    queſtioned ſo,
  And ſwore by Pan it was not for his
    flocks ;
' 'Tis love, fair Phillis, breedeth all this
    woe,
  My thoughts are trapt within thy
    lovely locks ;
Thine eye hath pierced, thy face hath
    ſet on fire ;
Fair Phillis kindleth Coridon's deſire.'

' Can ſhepherds love ?' ſaid Phillis to
    the ſwain :
  ' Such ſaints as Phillis,' Coridon re-
    plied :
' Men when they luſt can many fancies
    feign,'
  Said Phillis. This not Coridon de-
    nied,
        * *clownish, awkward.*

That luft had lies ; ' But love,' quoth
    he, ' fays truth :
Thy fhepherd loves, then, Phillis, what
    enfu'th ?'

Phillis was won : fhe blufhed and hung
    the head ;
    The fwain ftept to and cheered her
    with a kifs :
With faith, with troth, they ftruck the
    matter dead ;
    So ufèd they when men thought not
    amifs :
This love begun and ended both in one ;
Phillis was loved, and fhe liked Coridon.
    (' Perimedes' [1588], vii., pp. 91, 92.)

PASTORAL.

The Shepherd's Wife's Song.

Ah, what is love ?   It is a pretty thing,
As fweet unto a fhepherd as a king,
      And fweeter too ;
For kings have cares that wait upon a
    crown,
And cares can make the fweeteft love to
    frown :
      Ah then, ah then,

If country loves fuch fweet defires do
    gain,
What lady would not love a fhepherd
    fwain ?

His flocks are folded, he comes home at
    night,
As merry as a king in his delight,
        And merrier too ;
For kings bethink them what the State
    require,
Where fhepherds carelefs carol by the
    fire :
        Ah then, ah then,
If country loves fuch fweet defires do
    gain,
What lady would not love a fhepherd
    fwain ?

He kiffeth firft, then fits as blithe to
    eat
His cream and curds as doth the king
    his meat,
        And blither too ;
For kings have often fears when they
    do fup,
Where fhepherds dread no poifon in
    their cup :
        Ah then, ah then,

If country loves fuch fweet defires do
 gain,
What lady would not love a fhepherd
 fwain ?

To bed he goes, as wanton then, I
 ween,
As is a king in dalliance with a queen,
   More wanton too ;
For kings have many griefs affects* to
 move,
Where fhepherds have no greater grief
 than love :
   Ah then, ah then,
If country loves fuch fweet defires do
 gain,
What lady would not love a fhepherd
 fwain ?

Upon his couch of ftraw he fleeps as
 found
As doth the king upon his bed of down,
   More founder too ;
For cares caufe kings full oft their fleep
 to fpill,†
Where weary fhepherds lie and fnort
 their fill :
   Ah then, ah then,

  * *affection.*   † *spoil.*

If country loves ſuch ſweet deſires do
    gain,
What lady would not love a ſhepherd
    ſwain ?

Thus with his wife he ſpends the year,
    as blithe
As doth the king at every tide or ſithe,*
    And blither too ;
For kings have wars and broils to take
    in hand,
Where ſhepherds laugh and love upon
    the land :
    Ah then, ah then,
If country loves ſuch ſweet deſires do
    gain,
What lady would not love a ſhepherd
    ſwain ?

* Query 'tide'=Christmas-tide ? ; 'sithe '
not simply 'time,' but = scythe = Harvest ?—
G.

PASTORAL.

Radagon in Dianem.

It was a valley gaudy-green,
Where Dian at the fount was feen ;
  Green it was,
  And did 'pafs
All other of Diana's bowers
In the pride of Flora's flowers.

A fount it was that no fun fees,
Circled in with cyprefs-trees,
  Set fo nigh
  As Phœbus' eye
Could not do the virgins fcathe,
To fee them naked when they bathe.

She fat there all in white,—
Colour fitting her delight :
  Virgins fo
  Ought to go,
For white in armory is placed
To be the colour that is chafte.

Her taff'ta caffock you might fee
Tucked up above her knee ;
  Which did fhow
  There below
Legs as white as whalès-bone ;
So white and chafte were never none.

Hard by her, upon the ground,
Sat her virgins in a round,
      Bathing their
      Golden hair,
And finging all in notes high,
' Fie on Venus' flattering eye !'

' Fie on love ! It is a toy ;
Cupid witlefs and a boy ;
      All his fires,
      And defires,
Are plagues that God fent down from
    high,
To pefter men with mifery.

As thus the virgins did difdain
Lovers' joy and lovers' pain,
      Cupid nigh
      Did efpy,
Grieving at Diana's fong ;
Slyly ftole thefe maids among.

His bow of fteel, darts of fire,
He fhot amongft them fweet defire ;
      Which ftraight flies
      In their eyes,
And at the entrance made them ftart,
For it ran from eye to heart.

Califto ftraight fuppofèd Jove
Was fair and frolic for to love ;
      Dian fhe
      'Scaped not free ;
For well I wot, hereupon
She loved the fwain Endymion.

Clytie Phœbus, and Chloris' eye
Thought none fo fair as Mercury :
      Venus thus
      Did difcufs,
By her fon in darts of fire,
None fo chafte to check defire.

Dian rofe with all her maids,
Blufhing thus at love's braids :*
      With fighs, all
      Show their thrall ;
And flinging hence pronounce this faw,
' What fo ftrong as love's fweet law ?'
    (' Francifco's Fortunes, or Second Part
      of Never too Late ' [1590], viii.,
      pp. 212-214.)

  * Dyce annotates ' *i.e.*, perhaps crafts, de-
ceits (*vide* Steeven's note on " Since French-
men are so *braid*," Shakespeare's " All's Well
that Ends Well," Act IV., Sc. ii.).' But surely
the word is simply 'braids = upbraids or up-
braidings, as 'pass for surpass, 'gan for began,
etc., etc.—G.

PASTORAL.

Philomela's Ode that she sung in her Arbour.

Sitting by a river's side,
Where a silent stream did glide,
Muse I did of many things
That the mind in quiet brings.
I 'gan think how some men deem
Gold their god; and some esteem
Honour is the chief content
That to man in life is lent;
And some others do contend
Quiet none like to a friend;
Others hold, there is no wealth
Compared to a perfect health;
Some man's mind in quiet stands
When he is lord of many lands:
But I did sigh, and said all this
Was but a shade of perfect bliss;
And in my thoughts I did approve
Naught so sweet as is true love.
Love 'twixt lovers, passeth these,
When mouth kisseth and heart 'grees;
With folded arms and lips meeting,
Each soul another sweetly greeting:
For by the breath the soul fleeteth,
And soul with soul in kissing meeteth!

If love be fo fweet a thing
That fuch happy blifs doth bring,
Happy is love's fugared thrall ;
But unhappy maidens all,
Who eftccm your virgin bliffes
Sweeter than a wife's fweet kiffes.
No fuch quiet to the mind
As true love with kiffes kind :
But if a kifs prove unchafte
Then is true love quite difgraced.
    Though love be fweet, learn this
      of me,
    No love fweet but honefty.
('Philomela, the Lady Fitzwalter's Night-
ingale' [1592], xi., pp. 123, 124.)

PASTORAL.

Philomela's Second Ode.

It was frofty winter-feafon,
And fair Flora's wealth was geafon.*
Meads that erft with green were fpread,
With choice flowers diap'red,

* My friend Mr. A. H. Bullen (' Lyrics from
Elizabethan Romances ') annotates = rare, un-
common.   Such is *a* meaning of the word, but
not the meaning here.   It is = parched, dried
up—as a well is said to be geasoned when it is
dry.—G.

Had tawny veils ; cold had scanted
What the Spring and Nature planted.
Leafless boughs there might you see,
All except fair Daphne's tree :
On their twigs no birds perched ;
Warmer coverts now they searched ;
And by Nature's secret reason
Framed their voices to the season,
With their feeble tunes bewraying
How they grieved the Spring's decaying.
Frosty Winter thus had gloomed
Each fair thing that Summer bloomed ;
Fields were bare, and trees unclad,
Flowers withered, birds were sad ;
When I saw a shepherd fold
Sheep in cote, to shun the cold ;
Himself sitting on the grass
That with the frost withered was,
Sighing deeply, thus 'gan say ;
' Love is folly when astray :
Like to love no passion such,
For 'tis madness, if too much ;
If too little, then despair ;
If too high, he beats the air
With bootless cries ; if too low,
An eagle matcheth with a crow :
Thence grow jars. Thus I find,
Love is folly, if unkind ;
Yet do men most desire

To be heated with this fire,
Whose flame is so pleasing hot
That they burn, yet feel it not.
Yet hath love another kind,
Worse than these unto the mind ;
That is, when a wanton eye
Leads desire clean awry,
And with the bee doth rejoice
Every minute to change choice ;
Counting he were then in bliss
If that each fair face were his.
Highly thus is love disgrac'd
When the lover is unchaste,
And would taste of fruit forbidden,
'Cause the 'scape is easily hidden.
Though such love be sweet in brewing,
Bitter is the end ensuing ;
For the honour of love he shameth,
And himself with lust defameth ;
For a minute's pleasure-gaining,
Fame and honour ever staining.
Gazing thus so far awry,
Last the chip falls in his eye ;
Then it burns that erst but heat him ;
And his own rod 'gins to beat him ;
His choicest sweets turn to gall ;
He finds lust is sin's thrall ;
That wanton women in their eyes
Men's deceivings do comprise ;

That homage done to fair faces
Doth difhonour other graces.
If lawlefs love be fuch a fin,
Curfed is he that lives therein ;
For the gain of Venus' game
Is the downfall unto fhame.'
    Here he paufèd, and did ftay,
Sighed, and rofe, and went away.
        (' Philomela,' xi., pp. 133-135.)

*ISABELL'S ODE.**

Sitting by a river fide,
Where a filent ftream did glide,
Bank'd about with choice flowers,
Such as fpring from April fhowers,
When fair Iris fmiling fhews
All her riches in her dews :
Thick-leaved trees fo were planted
As nor Art nor Nature wanted :

* It will be observed that Philomela's Ode,
that precedes this, opens with the same
couplet. Even my friend Mr. A. H. Bullen
seems to have overlooked this Ode because of
this, and so omitted it in his selections, etc.
('Lyrics from Elizabethan Romances'), but
even he shows by his actual selections per-
functory acquaintance with Greene and others.
—G.

Bord'ring all the brook with fhade
As if Venus there had made
By Flora's wile a curious bower
To dally with her paramour.
  At this current as I gaz'd,
Eyes entrapp'd, mind amaz'd ;
I might fee in my ken
Such a flame as fireth men :
Such a fire as doth fry
With one blaze both heart and eye :
Such a heat as doth prove
No heat like to heat of love.
Bright fhe was, for 'twas a fhe
That traced her fteps towards me ;
On her head fhe wore a bay,
To fence Phœbus' light away :
In her face one might defcry
The curious beauty of the fky ;
Her eyes carried darts of fire,
Feather'd all with fwift defire ;
Yet forth thefe fiery darts did pafs
Pearled tears as bright as glafs ;
That wonder 'twas in her eyne
Fire and water fhould combine :
If th' old faw did not borrow
Fire is love and water forrow.
Down fhe fate, pale and fad,
No mirth in her looks fhe had :
Face and eyes fhowed diftrefs,

Inward fighs difcourf'd no lefs :
Head on hand might I fee,
Elbow leanèd on her knee ;
Laft fhe breathed out this faw,
' Oh, that love hath no law !'
Love enforceth with conftraint,
Love delighteth in complaint ;
Whofo loves hates his life,
For love's peace is mind's ftrife ;
Love doth feed on beauty's fare,
Every difh fauc'd with care :
Chiefly women, reafon why,
Love is hatch'd in their eye ;
Thence it fteppeth to the heart,
There it poifoneth every part :
Mind and heart, eye and thought,
Till fweet love their woes hath wrought:
Then repentant they 'gan cry,
' Oh, my heart that trow'd* mine eye !'
    Thus fhe faid, and then fhe rofe,
Face and mind both full of woes ;
Flinging thence, with this faw,
Fie on love that hath no law.
      (' Never too Late,' viii., pp. 50-52.)

---

* *trusted, held for true.*

PASTORAL.

Francesco's Ode.

When I look about the place
Where forrow nurfeth up difgrace ;
Wrapt within a fold of cares,
Whofe diftrefs no heart fpares :
Eyes might look, but fee no light,
Heart might think but on defpite :
Sun did fhine, but not on me,
Sorrow faid it may not be,
That heart or eye fhould once poffefs
Any falve to cure diftrefs :
For men in prifon muft fuppofe
Their couches are the beds of woes.
Seeing this I fighèd then,
Fortune thus fhould punifh men.
But when I call'd to mind her face
For whofe love I brook this place ;
Starry eyes, whereat my fight
Did eclipfe with much delight ;
Eyes that lighten and do fhine,
Beams of love that are divine ;
Lily cheeks whereon befide
Buds of rofes fhew their pride ;
Cherry lips, which did fpeak
Words that made all hearts to break :
Words moft fweet, for breath was fweet ;

Such perfume for love is meet.
Precious words, as hard to tell
Which more pleafed, wit or fmell :
When I faw my greateft pains
Grow for her that beauty ftains ;
Fortune thus I did reprove.—
Nothing grievefull grows from Love.
(Ibid., pp. 62-63.)

PASTORAL.

Doron's Jig.

Through the fhrubs as I 'gan crack
    For my lamb's little ones,
    'Mongft many pretty ones,
Nymphs I mean, whofe hair was black
        As the crow :
        Like the fnow
Her face and brows fhin'd, I ween ;
    I faw a little one,
    A bonny pretty one,
As bright, buxom, and as fheen
        As was fhe
        On her knee,

That lull'd the god, whofe arrows warms:
    Such merry little ones,
    Such fair-fac'd pretty ones,
As dally in Love's chiefeft harms ;
    Such was mine ;
    Whofe gray eyne
Made me love. I 'gan to woo
    This fweet little one,
    This bonny pretty one ;
I woo'd hard a day or two ;
            Till fhe bad,
            Be not fad ;
Woo no more, I am thine own,
    Thy deareft little one,
    Thy trueft pretty one ;
Thus was faith and firm love fhown,
            As behoves
            Shepherds' loves.
    (' Menaphon ' [1589], vi., pp. 69, 70.)

PERSEVERANCE WINS.

    I now, quoth fhe, both fee and try
by experience, that there is no fifh fo
fickle but will come to the bait ; no
doe fo wild but will ftand at the gaze* ;
          * *staring.*

no hawk ſo haggard* but will ſtoop to
the lure ; no nieſſet† ſo ramage‡ but will
be reclaimed to the lunes ; no fruit ſo
fine but the caterpillar will conſume it ;
no adamant§ ſo hard but will yield to
the file ; . . . no maid ſo free but love
will bring her to bondage and thraldom.
('Card of Fancy' [1587], iv., p. 120.)
[On the word 'lunes' the Shakeſpeare
ſtudent will do well to conſult a full note
in Works, vol. ii., pp. 330-333, and Gloſ-
ſarial Index (in vol. xv.)—one of multi-
plied inſtances of Greene's words and
phraſing ſhedding light on obſcurities
and cruxes of Shakeſpeare.—G.]

WORD-PORTRAITS.

Ovid.

Quaint was Ovid in his rhyme,
Chiefeſt poet of his time :
What he could in words rehearſe
Ended in a pleaſing verſe :

* *untrained.*	† *hawk.*
‡ *wild.*	§ *diamond.*

Apollo with his aye-green bays
Crown'd his head to show his praise;
And all the Muses did agree
He should be theirs, and none but he.
  This Poet chanted all of Love,
Of Cupid's wings and Venus' dove;
Of fair Corinna and her hue,
Of white and red and veins blue.
How they lov'd and how they 'greed,
And how in fancy they did speed.
  His Elegies were wanton all,
Telling of Love's pleasing thrall,
And 'cause he would the Poet seem,
That best of Venus' laws could deem,
Strange precepts he did impart,
And writ three books of Love's art;
There he taught how to woo,
What in love men should do;
How they might soonest win
Honest women unto sin:
Thus to tellen all the truth
He infected Rome's youth,
And with his books and verses brought
That men in Rome nought else sought
But how to 'tangle maid or wife,
With honour's breach through wanton
      life;
The foolish sort did for his skill
Praise the deepness of his quill,

And like to him faid there was none
Since died old Anacreon.
But Rome's Auguftus, world's wonder,
Brook'd not of this foolifh blunder ;
Nor lik'd he of this wanton verfe
That Love's laws did rehearfe ;
For well he faw and did efpy
Youth was fore impair'd thereby ;
And by experience he finds
Wanton books infeЄt the minds ;
Which made him ftraight for reward,
Though the cenfure* ·feemèd hard
To banifh Ovid quite from Rome,
This was great Auguftus' doom ;
For (quoth he) Poets' quills
Ought not for to teach men ills ;
For learning is a thing of praife,
To fhow precepts to make men wife ;
And near the Mufes' facred places
Dwells the virtuous-minded graces.
'Tis fhame and fin, then, for good wits
To fhow their fkill in wanton fits.
This Auguftus did reply.
And as he faid, ·fo think I.
     ('Greene's Vifion' [1592], xii., pp.
         199-201.)

* *judgment.*

The Description of Sir Geoffrey Chaucer.

His ftature was not very tall ;
Lean he was ; his legs were fmall,
Hofed within a ftock of red ;
A button'd bonnet on his head,
From under which did hang, I ween,
Silver hairs both bright and fheen ;
His beard was white, trimmèd round,
His countenance blithe and merry
    found :
A fleevelefs jacket large and wide,
With many plaits and fkirts' fide,
Of water chamlet* did he wear
A whittell† by his belt he bear.
His fhoes were corned,‡ broad before ;
His inkhorn at his fide he wore ;
And in his hand he bore a book ;
Thus did this ancient poet look.
          (*Ibid.*, pp. 209-210.)

* *camel's hair cloth, rain-proof.—G.*
† *clasp-knife.*
‡ *projecting = cornered.*

John Gower.

Large he was, his height was long ;
Broad of breaſt, his limbs were ſtrong ;
But colour pale, and wan his look,—
Such have they that plyen their book :
His head was gray and quaintly ſhorn ;
Neatly was his beard worn ;
His viſage grave, ſtern and grim,—
Cato was moſt like to him.
His bonnet was a hat of blue,
His ſleeves ſtraight, of that ſame hue ;
A ſurcoat* of a tawny dye,
Hung in plaits over his thigh ;
A breech cloſe unto his dock,
Handſom'd with a long ſtock ;
Pricked before were his ſhoon,
He wore ſuch as others doon :
A bag of red by his ſide,
And by that his napkin tied :
Thus John Gower did appear,
Quaint attirèd, as you hear.
                    (*Ibid.,* p. 210.)

* *outer garment.*

Solomon.

His ftature tall, large, and high,
Limb'd and featur'd beauteoufly ;
Cheft was broad, arms were ftrong,
Locks of amber paffing long,
That hung and wav'd upon his neck,
Heaven's beauty might they check.
Vifage fair and full of grace,
Mild and ftern, for in one place
Sate Mercy meekly in his eye,
And juftice in his looks hard bye :
His robes of biffe* were crimfon hue,
Bordered round with twines of blue :
In Tyre no richer filk fold,
Over-braided all with gold ;
Coftly fet with precious ftone,
Such before I ne'er faw none :
A maffy crown upon his head,
Chequer'd through with rubies red ;
Orient pearl and bright topace†
Did burnifh out each valiant place :
Thus this Prince that feemèd fage
Did go in royal equipage.

(Ibid., p. 275.)

* *fine silk.* † *topaz.*

POTATOES.

[Licentiousness works wastefully] . . .
the apothecaries would have surphaling
water and potato roots lie dead on their
hands. ('Disputation between a Hee and
Shee Conny-Catcher [1592], x., 234.)
[Surphaling, *i.e.*, a cosmetic wash. It
is odd to find potatoes in apothecaries'
shops. They were then held to be
provocatives. They had not long been
introduced into England.—G.]

TIME.

In time we see the silver drops
    The craggy stones make soft ;
The slowest snail in time we see
    Doth creep and climb aloft.

With feeble puffs the tallest pine
    In tract of time doth fall ;
The hardest heart in time doth yield
    To Venus' luring call.

Where chilling frost alate did nip
    There flasheth now a fire ;
Where deep disdain bred noisome hate,
    There kindleth now desire.

Time caufeth hope to have his hap :
  What care in time not eafed ?
In time I loathed that now I love ;
  In both content and pleafed.
    ('Arbafto' [1584], iii., p. 248.)

THE TONGUE.

It feemeth (faith Bias) that Nature by fortifying the tongue would teach how precious and neceffary a virtue filence is ; for fhe hath placed before it the bulwark of the teeth, that if it will not obey reafon, which being within ought to ferve inftead of a bridle to ftay it from preventing the thoughts, we might reftrain and chaftife fuch impudent babbling by biting. And, therefore, faith he, we have two eyes and two ears, that thereby we may learn to hear and fee much more than is fpoken.
    ('Penelope's Web,' v., p. 221.)

Invective on Contemporaries.

I am not ignorant how eloquent our gowned age is grown of late ; fo that every mechanical mate abhors the Englifh he was born to, and plucks with a folemn periphrafis his *ut vales* from the inkhorn ; which I impute not fo much to the perfection of arts as to the fervile imitation of vainglorious tragedians, who contend not fo ferioufly to excel in action as to embowel the clouds in a fpeech of comparifon ; thinking themfelves more than initiated in poets' immortality if they but once get Boreas by the beard and the heavenly Bull by the dew-lap. But herein I cannot fo fully bequeath them to folly as their idiot art-mafters, that intrude themfelves to our ears as the alchymifts of eloquence : who (mounted on the ftage of arrogance) think to outbrave better pens with the fwelling bombaft of a bragging blank verfe. Indeed, it may be the ingrafted overflow of fome kil-cow* conceit, that overcloyeth their imagination with a more than drunken refolution, being not extemporal in the

* =a butcher—query a disguised gird at Shakespeare the wool-stapler's son ?—G.

invention of any other means to vent their manhood, commits the digeſtion of their choleric encumbrances to the ſpacious volubility of a drumming de-caſillabon. 'Mongſt this kind of men that repoſe eternity in the mouth of a player, I can but engroſs ſome deep-read grammarians, who having no more learning in their ſkull than will ſerve to take up a commodity, nor art in their brain, than was nouriſhed in a ſerving-man's idleneſs, will take upon them to be the ironical cenſors of all, when God and Poetry doth know, they are the ſimpleſt of all. To leave theſe to the mercy of their mother-tongue, that feed on nought but the crumbs that fall from the tranſlator's trencher, I come (ſweet friend) to thy Arcadian 'Menaphon.' . . . (Naſhe's Epiſtle to the Gentlemen Students of both Univerſities . . . pre-fixed to 'Menaphon' [1589], vi., pp. 9, 10.) [This is given to ſhow Naſhe's fellow-feeling with Greene.—G.]

TRAVELS.

In my opinion the fitteft kind of life for a young gentleman to take (who as yet hath not fubdued the youthful conceits of fancy nor made a conqueft of his will by wit) is to fpend his time in travel; wherein he fhall find both pleafure and profit : yea, and buy that by experience which otherwife with all the treafure in the world he cannot purchafe. For what changeth vanity to virtue, ftaylefs wit to ftayed wifdom, fond fantafies to firm affections, but travel ? What repreffeth the rage of youth and redreffeth the witlefs fury of wanton years, but travel ? What turneth a fecure life to a careful living ? What maketh the foolifh wife ? yea, what increafeth wit and augmenteth fkill, but travel? in fo much that the fame Ulyffes won was not by the ten years he lay at Troy, but by the time he fpent in travel.

('Card of Fancy' [1587], iv., p. 19.)

USURY.

Enter the Ufurer folus with a halter in one hand, a dagger in the other.

Groaning in confcience, burdened with
    my crimes,
The hell of forrow haunts me up and
    down ;
Tread where I lift, methinks the bleed-
    ing ghofts
Of thofe whom my corruption brought
    to nought,
Do ferve for ftumbling-blocks before
    my fteps ;
The fatherlefs and widow wronged by
    me,
The poor oppreffèd by my ufury ;
Methinks I fee their hands rear'd up to
    heaven,
To cry for vengeance of my covetoufnefs.
Wherefo I walk, all figh and fhun my
    way ;
Thus I am made a monfter of the world ;
Hell gapes for me, heaven will not hold
    my foul.
You mountains, fhroud me from the
    God of truth ;
Methinks I fee Him fit to judge the
    earth ;

See how He blots me out of the book of
    life :
Oh burden more than Ætna, that I
    bear.
Cover me, hills, and ſhroud me from the
    Lord ;
Swallow me, Lycus, ſhield me from the
    Lord.
In life no peace ; each murmuring that
    I hear
Methinks the ſentence of damnation
    ſounds,
'Die, reprobate, and hie thee hence to
    hell.'
    ('A Looking-glaſs for London and
    England' [1594], xiv., pp. 97, 98.)

VENGEANCE IMPLORED.

*Prince Aga, his eyes put out and hands
cut off by Acomat.*

. . . Oh Thou ſupreme Architect of all,
Firſt Mover of thoſe tenfold cryſtal orbs,
Where all thoſe moving and unmoving
    eyes

Behold Thy goodnefs everlaftingly ;
See, unto Thee I lift thefe bloody arms :
For hands I have not for to lift to Thee ;
And in Thy juftice dart thy fmould'ring
    flame
Upon the head of curfèd Acomat.
Oh cruel heavens and injurious fates !
Even the laft refuge of a wretched man
Is took from me ; for how can Aga
    weep ?
Or run a brinifh fhower of pearled tears,
Wanting the watery cifterns of his eyes ?
    Come, lead me back again to Bajazet,
The wofulleft and faddeft ambaffador
That ever was defpatched to any king.
        ('Selimus,' xiv., p. 247.)

VENUS AND ADONIS.

In Cyprus fat fair Venus by a fount,
  Wanton Adonis toying on her knee ;
She kiffed the wag, her darling of
    account ;
  The boy 'gan blufh ; which when his
    lover fee,

She fmiled, and told him love might
    challenge debt,
And he was young, and might be wanton
    yet.

The boy waxed bold, fired by fond defire,
    That woo he could and court her
      with conceit :
Reafon fpied this, and fought to quench
    the fire
    With cold difdain ; but wily Adon
      ftraight
Cheered up the flame, and faid : ' Good
    fir, what let ?*
I am but young, and may be wanton
    yet.'

Reafon replied, that beauty was a bane
    To fuch as feed their fancy with fond
      love ;
That when fweet youth with luft is
    overta'en,
    It rues in age ; this could not Adon
      move,
For Venus taught him ftill this reft to
    fet,†
That he was young, and might be
    wanton yet.

* *hindrance.*
† a term used in the game of primero.—G.

Where Venus ſtrikes with beauty to the
  quick,
  It little 'vails ſage Reaſon to reply ;
Few are the cures for ſuch as are love-
  ſick,
  But love : then, though I wanton it
  awry,
And play the wag, from Adon this I
  get,—
I am but young, and may be wanton yet.
  ('Perimedes the Blackſmith' [1588],
  vii., pp. 88, 89.)

ADONIS REPROVED.

The ſiren Venus nouriced* in her lap,
  Fair Adon, ſwearing whiles he was a
  youth
He might be wanton ; note his after-
  hap,
  The guerdon that ſuch lawleſs luſt
  enfu'th ;
So long he followed flattering Venus'
  lore,
Till, ſilly lad, he periſhed by a boar.†

* *nursed.*   † the classical myth.—G.

Mars in his youth did court this lufty
    dame ;
  He won her love ; what might his
    fancy let ?*
He was but young : at laft unto his
    fhame
  Vulcan entrapped them flyly in a net ;
And called the gods to witnefs as a truth
A lecher's fault was not excufed by
    youth.

If crooked age accounteth youth his
    Spring,
  The Spring, the faireft feafon of the
    year ;
Enriched with flowers, and fweets, and
    many a thing
  That fair and gorgeous to the eyes
    appear ;
It fits that youth, the Spring of man,
    fhould be
'Riched with fuch flowers as virtue
    yieldeth thee.
              (*Ibid.*, vii., pp. 89, 90.)

* *hinder.*

VENUS VICTRIX.

Mars in a fury 'gainſt Love's brighteſt
    Queen,
    Put on his helm', and took to him his
      lance ;
On Erycinus Mount* was Mavors ſeen,
    And there his enſigns did the god
      advance ;
And by heaven's greateſt gates he ſtoutly
    ſwore,
Venus ſhould die, for ſhe had wronged
    him ſore.

Cupid heard this, and he began to cry,
    And wiſhed his mother's abſence for
      awhile :
'Peace, fool,' quoth Venus ; 'Is it I
    muſt die ?
    Muſt it be, Mars ?' With that ſhe
    coined a ſmile ;
She trimmed her treſſes, and did curl
    her hair,
And made her face with beauty paſſing
    fair.

* The mountain from which Venus received
the name of Erycina was Eryx. But Greene
and his contemporaries spelled Erycinus.—G.

P 2

A fan of filver feathers in her hand,
   And in a coach of ebony fhe went:
She paffed the place where furious Mars
     did ftand,
   And out her looks a lovely fmile fhe
     fent;
Then from her brows leaped out fo
     fharp a frown,
That Mars for fear threw all his armour
     down.

He vowed repentance for his rafh mif-
     deed,
   Blaming his choler that had caufed
     his woe:
Venus grew gracious, and with him
     agreed,
   But charged him not to threaten
     beauty fo;
For women's looks are fuch enchanting
     charms
As can fubdue the greateft god in
     arms.
   ('Ciceronis Amor' [1589], vii., pp.
     133, 134.)

WOMAN.

Difcourteous women, Nature's faireft ill,
The woe of man, that firft created curfe,
Bafe female fex, fprung from black Ates'
loins,
Proud and difdainful, cruel and unjuft ;
Whofe words are fhaded with enchant-
ing wiles
Worfe than Medufa, mateth* all our
minds :
And in their heart fits fhamelefs treachery,
Turning a truthlefs, vile circumference.
O, could my fury paint their furies
forth !
For hell's no hell, compared to their
hearts ;
Too fimple devils to conceal their arts ;
Born to be plagues unto the thoughts
of men ;
Brought for eternal peftilence to the
world.
(' Orlando Furiofo,' xiii., pp. 149, 150.)

* *confounds.*

Woman—compared to a Rofe.

Marry, . . . I can aptly compare a woman to a Rofe : for as we cannot enjoy the fragrant fmell of the one without fharp prickles, fo we cannot poffefs the virtues of the other without fhrewifh conditions ; and yet neither the one nor the other can well be forborne, for they are neceffary evils. (' Morando ' [1587], iii., p. 101.)

Comparifons Defcriptive of a Fair Woman (Sepheftia).

All this while Menaphon fate amongft the fhrubs, fixing his eyes on the glorious objeɛt of her face : he noted her treffes, which he compared to the coloured hyacinth of Arcadia ; her brows to the mountain fnows that lie on the hills ; her eyes to the gray glifter of Titan's gorgeous mantle ; her alabafter neck to the whitenefs of his flocks ; her teeth to pearl ; her face to borders of lilies interfeamed with rofes : to be brief, our shepherd Menaphon, that heretofore was an atheist to love, and as the Thessalian of Bacchus, so he, a contemner of Venus, was now by the wily shaft of Cupid so entangled in the perfection and beauteous excellence of Sepheftia, as now he swore no benign planet but Venus, no god but Cupid, nor exquisite deity but Love. ('Menaphon' [1589], vi., p. 49.)

An only Daughter.

One only daughter of such excellent exquisite perfection as Nature in her seemed to wonder at her own works. Her hair was like the shine of Apollo, when, shaking his glorious tresses, he makes the world beauteous with his brightness. The ivory of her face overdashed with a vermilion dye, seemed like the blush that leapt from Endymion's cheeks when Cynthia courts him on the hills of Latmos. ('Ciceronis Amor' [1589], vii., pp. 105, 106.)

    Green Pastures.

THE YEOMAN AND PEASANTRY OF OLD ENGLAND.*

Enter the Juſtice, a townſman [of Wake-field], George a Greene, and Sir Nicholas Mannering with his commiſſion.

Juſtice. Maſter Mannering, ſtand aſide
    whilſt we confer
What is beſt to do. Townſmen of
    Wakefield,
The Earl of Kendal here hath ſent for
    victuals,
And in aiding him we ſhow ourſelves
    no leſs
Than traitors to the king : therefore
Let me hear, townſmen, what is your
    conſents.
    Firſt townſman. Even as you pleaſe,
      we are all content.
    Juſtice. Then, Maſter Mannering, we
      are reſolved.
    Man. As how ?
    Juſtice. Marry, Sir, thus.—
We will ſend the Earl of Kendal no
    victuals,

---

* Greene's portrayal of country life and siding with the commonalty is extremely noticeable. See Life prefixed to his Works, as before.—G.

Becaufe he is a traitor to the king ;
And in aiding him we'd fhow ourfelves
    no lefs.
    Man. Why, men of Wakefield, are
    you waxen mad,
That prefent danger cannot whet your
    wits,
Wifely to make provifion of yourfelves ?
The Earl is thirty thoufand men, ftrong
    in power,
And what town fo ever him refift
He lays it flat and level with the ground:
Ye filly men, you feek your own decay :
Therefore fend my lord fuch provifion
    as he wants,
So he will fpare your town
And come no nearer Wakefield than he is.
    Juftice. Mafter Mannering, you have
    your anfwer,
You may be gone.
    Man. Well, Woodroffe, for fo I guefs
    is thy name,
I'll make thee curfe thy overthwart
    denial ;
And all that fit upon the bench this day
Shall rue the hour they have withftood
My Lord's commiffion.
    Juftice. Do thy worft, we fear thee
    not.

Man. See you thefe fcals? Before
 you pafs the town
I will have all things my lord doth
 want,
In fpite of you.
 George a Greene. Proud dapper Jack,
 vail bonnet to the bench
That reprefents the perfon of the king;
Or, firrha, I'll lay thy head before thy
 feet.
 Man. Why, who art thou?
 George. Why, I am George a Greene,
True liegeman to my king;
Who fcorns that men of fuch efteem as
 thefe,
Should brook the braves of any traitorous
 fquire:
You of the bench, and you, my fellow
 friends,
Neighbours, are fubjects all unto the
 king;
We are Englifh born, and therefore
 Edward's friends,
Vowed unto him even in our mother's
 womb;
Our minds to God, our hearts unto our
 king,
Our wealth, our homage, and our car-
 cafes,

Be all King Edward's : then, firrha, we
    have
Nothing left for traitors but our fwords,
Whetted to bathe them in your bloods,
    and die
'Gainft you, before we fend you any
    victuals.
    Juftice. Well fpoken, George a
    Greene.
    Firft townfman. Pray let George a
    Greene fpeak for us.
    George. Sirrha, you get no victuals
    here,
Not if a hoof of beef would fave your
    lives.
    Man. Fellow, I ftand amaz'd at thy
    prefumption :
Why, what art thou that dareft gainfay
    my lord,
Knowing his mighty puiffance and his
    ftroke ?
Why, my friend, I come not barely of
    myfelf ;
For fee, I have a large commiffion.
    George. Let me fee it, firrha.
              [*Takes the commiffion.*
Whofe feals be thefe ?
    Man. This is the Earl of Kendal's
    feal at arms ;

This Lord Charnel Bonfield's ;
And this Sir Gilbert Armftrong's.
   George. I tell thee, firrha, did good
     King Edward's fon
Seal a commiffion 'gainft the King his
   father,
Thus would I tear it in defpite of him.
          [*He tears the commiffion.*
Being traitor to my fovereign.
   Man. What ?   Haft thou torn my
     lord's commiffion ?
Thou fhalt rue it, and fo fhall all Wake-
   field.
   George. What, are you in choler ? I
     will give you pills
To cool your ftomach. Seeft thou thefe
   feals ?
Now by my father's foul,
Which was a yeoman when he was alive ;
Eat them, or eat my dagger's point,
   proud fquire.
   Man. But thou doft but jeft, I hope.
   George. Sure that fhall you fee before
     we two part.
   Man. Well, an' there be no remedy,
   fo, George.
       [*Swallows one of the feals.*
One is gone : I pray thee no more
   now.

George. O, Sir,
If one be good, the others cannot
    hurt ;
So, Sir.
    [*Mannering swallows the other two seals.*
Now you may go and tell the Earl of
    Kendal,
Although I have rent his large com-
    miffion,
Yet of courtefy I have fent all his feals
Back again by you.
    Man. Well, Sir, I will do your errand.
                     [*Exit.*
    George. Now let him tell his lord,
    that he hath fpoke
With George a Greene,
Hight Pinner of merry Wakefield town;
That hath phyfic for a fool,
Pills for a traitor, that doth wrong his
    fovereign :
Are you content with this that I have
    done ?
    Juftice. Ay, content, George :
For highly haft thou honoured Wakefield
    town,
In cutting of proud Mannering fo
    fhort.
Come, thou fhalt be my welcome gueft
    to-day ;

Q

For well thou haſt deſerved reward and
favour.   [*Exeunt omnes.*
('The Pinner of Wakefield' [1599],
xiv., pp. 124-129.)

YOUTH DEGENERATE.

Youth, which in the golden age delighted to try their virtues in hard
armours, take their only content in
delicate and effeminate amours. ('Plane-
tomachia' [1585], v., p. 39.)

WOMAN'S EYES.

A Queſtion.

On women Nature did beſtow two eyes,
  Like heaven's bright lamps in match-.
    leſs beauty ſhining ;
Whoſe beams do ſooneſt captivate the
    wiſe
  And wary heads made rare by Art's
    refining.
  But why did Nature in her choice
    combining

Plant two fair eyes within a beauteous
    face ?
That they might favour two with equal
    grace.
Venus did foothe up Vulcan with one eye,
    With th' other granted Mars his
    wifhèd glee ;
If fhe did fo who Hymen did defy,
    Think love no fin but grant an eye
    to me ;
    In vain elfe Nature gave two ftars to
    thee :
If then two eyes may well two friends
    maintain,
Allow of two, and prove not Nature
    vain.
    ('Philomela' [1592], xi., p. 142.

Anfwer.

Nature forefeeing how men would de-
    vife
    More wiles than Proteus, women to
    entice,
Granted them two, and thofe bright
    fhining eyes,
    To pierce into men's faults if they
    were wife ;
    For they with fhow of virtue mafk
    their vice :

Therefore to women's eyes belong these
  gifts,
The one must love, the other see men's
  shifts.
Both these await upon one simple heart,
  And what they choose, it hides up
    without change.
The emerald will not with his portrait
  part,
  Nor will a woman's thoughts delight
    to range;
  They hold it bad to have so bad
    exchange.
One heart, one friend, though that two
  eyes do choose him
No more but one, and heart will never
  lose him.

(*Ibid.*, p. 149.)

❦

THE DEAD WIFE SOON FORGOTTEN.

Lambert. Why, Serlsby, is thy wife so
  lately dead?
Are all thy loves so lightly passèd over,
As thou canst wed before the year be
  out?

Serlſby. I live not, Lambert, to content the dead,
Nor was I wedded but for life to her ;
The grave ends and begins a married
ſtate.

> ('Friar Bacon,' xiii., p. 70.)

THE END.